SEVEN DEAD

SEVEN DEAD

J. Jefferson Farjeon

With an Introduction by
MARTIN EDWARDS

This edition published 2017 by
The British Library
96 Euston Road
London NW1 2DB

Originally published in 1939 by Collins

Cataloguing in Publication Data

A catalogue record for this publication is
available from the British Library

ISBN 978 0 7123 5688 6

Typeset by Tetragon, London
Printed and bound by CPI Group (UK) Ltd, Croydon CR0 4YY

CONTENTS

INTRODUCTION

J. Jefferson Farjeon's most precious literary gift, his ability to conjure up atmospheric and compelling scenarios, was never more vividly displayed than in *Seven Dead*. It is a challenge to think of any opening situation in a crime novel more extraordinary than that which Ted Lyte discovers after climbing through a back window of Haven House. Ted is a petty thief and pickpocket who plucks up the courage to try his hand at housebreaking. One of the windows of the apparently deserted house is shuttered, and its door is closed, with a key in the lock. When he turns the key, he is greeted by a sight as shocking as it is bizarre.

Seven dead people, six men and one woman, are in the shuttered room, "revealed with a cruel starkness by the unnatural artificial light". Two of the men are dressed like sailors; the solitary female corpse is wearing a man's clothes: "She might have been attractive once. She was not attractive now." As Detective Inspector Kendall observes, "This has Madame Tussaud's beaten. I expect they'd like it for their Chamber of Horrors." As Kendall says, the seven people are "emaciated, filthily clothed, ill assorted, and with nothing on any of them to identify any one of them". The mystery deepens when a crumpled piece of paper is found, bearing an enigmatic message: *With apologies from the Suicide Club*. An even more cryptic clue is written in pencil on the other side of the sheet. And on the wall of the dining room hangs a picture of a pretty young girl—but a bullet has been put through her heart.

Kendall has been taken to the scene by Ted Lyte, in the company of a young man called Thomas Hazeldean whom Ted encountered during his terrified flight from Haven House. Kendall previously appeared in Farjeon's *Thirteen Guests*—another title in the British Library's series of Crime Classics—and Hazeldean contrasts him with the type of Great Detective so popular in the fiction of the time: "What I liked about him was that he didn't play the violin, or have a wooden leg, or anything of that sort. He just got on with it."

Kendall was, then, conceived as a relatively realistic police detective, rather as Farjeon's contemporary Freeman Wills Crofts conceived his series cop, Inspector Joseph French. But Farjeon was much less interested than Crofts in chronicling the minutiae of painstaking police procedure. His imagination was more vivid and romantic, and *Seven Dead* is by no means a conventional story of a police investigation. Much of the story focuses on Hazeldean's own search for the truth. This young fellow, a journalist and a yachtsman, is driven by his fascination with the girl in the picture. She is now a young woman, Dora Fenner, a member of the family which owns Haven House, and it seems that she has, for reasons unknown, fled across the Channel to Boulogne. On impulse, Hazeldean sails for France in the hope of finding her and solving the mystery.

Intriguingly, this concept of a sleuth who becomes obsessed with a painting of a young and beautiful member of the opposite sex resurfaced—just three years after *Seven Dead* was published—in a much more famous story, *Laura* by Vera Caspary, which in 1944 was adapted into a notable *film noir*. The two stories could scarcely be more different, but the coincidence is striking.

Seven Dead appeared at a time when Farjeon was at the peak of his popularity, but inevitably his reputation faded with the passage of time, and has only revived following the republication of titles such as *Mystery in White*, *Thirteen Guests* and *The Z Murders* in the Crime Classics series. One of the pleasures associated with my role as Series Consultant to the British Library has been the chance to talk to family members and others associated with the literary estates of writers of the past, and these discussions have expanded my knowledge and understanding of the lives and work of authors who certainly deserve to be remembered.

Joseph Jefferson Farjeon (1883–1955) is a case in point. His estate is now in the care of Edward Vandyck, who has kindly shared with me a memoir written by Alison Coate, who had a lifelong friendship with the Farjeon family, and in particular Joe Farjeon and his daughter Joan. Alison describes Farjeon—whose father, Benjamin, was himself a successful writer—as acutely sensitive, gentle, and unselfish, but also as a chronic worrier who was deeply troubled by the hatred he felt for his father's fiery outbursts of temper. Joe was a capable sportsman in his schooldays, with a particular love of cricket that is reflected in *Seven Dead* by the presence of a cricket ball in Haven House—yet another of the mysterious clues to the puzzle.

Prompted by his father, Joe Farjeon took up acting, but he soon realised that his nervous temperament was ill-suited to a career on the stage. He fell in love with an American girl, Frances Antoinette ("Fan") Wood, and they married in 1910; Joan was born three years later. He was deemed physically unfit for service in the First World War, and struggled to earn a living as a journalist before trying his hand at fiction and writing plays. He turned the corner as a result of the success of *No. 17*, a play that was filmed twice; he also later novelised it.

"Yet even at the height of his success", Alison Coates wrote, "Joe's fear of not being able to earn enough drove him on. He was rarely far from his typewriter." He became a prolific novelist, but kept striving to ensure that his standards never slipped, and was meticulous in checking his work for errors. His professionalism meant that his fiction was generally a cut above that of many of his peers, who were more willing to sacrifice quality in the pursuit of quantity. And, though his books were for many years out of print, there is an eternal appeal about the gift of storytelling, a gift which Joe Farjeon possessed in full measure—as this unorthodox mystery illustrates in the liveliest fashion.

MARTIN EDWARDS
www.martinedwardsbooks.com

CHAPTER I

Behind the Shutters

THIS IS NOT TED LYTE'S STORY. HE MERELY HAD THE EXCESSIVE misfortune to come into it, and to remain in it longer than he wanted. Had he adopted Cardinal Wolsey's advice and flung away ambition, continuing to limit his illegal acts to the petty pilfering and pickpocketing at which he was fairly expert, he would have spared himself on this historic Saturday morning the most horrible moment of his life. The moment was so horrible that it deprived him temporarily of his senses. But he was not a prophet; all he could predict of the future was the next instant, and that often wrongly; and the open gate, with the glimpse beyond of the shuttered window, tempted him.

He hadn't had much luck lately. He had been brooding on that dismal fact while searching for flotsam and jetsam along the deserted shore. Pretty well all he had found there was mud, and it was mud, coupled perhaps with the depressing sound of a fog-horn out at sea, that had driven him inland near Havenford Creek. But a shuttered window suggested brighter possibilities. It suggested an unoccupied house. If he could summon a little courage—it was lack of courage that prevented him from becoming a Napoleon of his trade—he might find a bit of all right behind those shutters! Wot abart it?

He glanced up and down the lane. The glance was satisfactory. Not a soul in sight. Not even a house—beyond this one. He glanced again at the open gate. It was swinging slightly on faintly squeaking hinges. Nasty sound. Almost as nasty as the fog-horn. Ted was susceptible to any form of nastiness just now, for it was a long while since his last square meal, and an empty stomach plays havoc with your manhood. Still, till you lived in a world where people looked after you, you had to work for your living.

So he took a breath and trespassed. Now he was beyond the gate, standing on gravel, and the gate was squeaking behind him instead of ahead of him. It was not nice smooth gravel. It was rough, with weeds growing out of it. It looped round an untidy plot of grass. You could go round whichever way you chose to the front porch—if you chose. Ted wasn't quite sure whether you chose. As he stared at the house, the house—two-storeyed, grey-bricked, half-dressed in dilapidated vines—stared back with one eye closed. The closed eye was the shuttered window on the right of the porch. There was no shutter over the window on the left. The uninvited guest got an unpleasant sensation that the house was winking at him.

Still, other signs were more favourable. There was no movement anywhere. There was no chimney-smoke. There was no dog. These omissions were too valuable to ignore in the state of the exchequer, and they decided him to take the risk. All that remained, therefore, was to find the way to get in.

He gave a quick glance behind him, to make sure that the short length of visible lane beyond the swinging gate was still empty, then hastened round the path to the porch. The front door, of course, was no good to him. Nor was the shuttered window. All the other windows in the front of the house were closed and locked, and he hesitated to break one till he had exhausted other less noisy possibilities. Not being a professional house-breaker, he had no implements to assist him. A professional could have sliced a circle out of the glass in a jiffy.

In the hope of finding an open window he went round the house. On the left was a narrow way between the wall and a high hedge, but somehow or other he didn't like the look of it, and chose a lawn on the right. The lawn stretched from the house to a long tangle of dark trees, and a french window opened on to it. The french window, like the window on the right of the front porch, was shuttered behind its glass.

"Wunner why they've shuttered one side of the 'ouse and not t'other?" ruminated Ted.

Had he known the reason, his knees would not have carried him any farther.

In happy ignorance, he passed the french window. The lawn, which needed scything, extended beyond the back of the house, ending at a little gate that led into a wood. Beyond the wood was the low cliff that dropped to Havenford Creek. But Ted was not interested in the scenery or the geography; it was the house itself that grimly fascinated him, and at the back, to his pleasant surprise, he found what he was looking for. A little window had not been securely fastened, and on being pushed inwards, it provided an aperture just large enough for a small man to slip through.

Ted was a small man, and fifteen seconds after the discovery he had dropped on to a scullery floor.

His first sensation was of intense relief. When you are breaking into a house you feel as though the whole world is watching you, but once you have entered, the world is shut outside. You pause for a few seconds to get back your breath and to enjoy the comforting privacy of close walls. To a man of Ted's fragile calibre, however, the sense of comfort is short-lived; and once he had fully realised that he had achieved his object of getting into the house, the next urgent object appeared to be to get out of it. Still, if he were ever to look himself in the face again, never the most cheering of occupations, he could not leave until he had secured some sort of a prize.

Sitting on his impulse to fly before the occasion demanded it, he stole softly out of the scullery. He did not need a plan of the house to find the larder. Instinct took him there, and appetite kept him there. For a few minutes Ted Lyte was completely happy. In fact, cheese and bread make such a difference to a man that when he emerged he did not see why he should not benefit by a handful of silver spoons as well. He knew a fellow who got rid of all the silver spoons you could find for him.

Leaving the larder quarters, he crept into the front hall. Here, ahead of him, was the front door at which he had stared so anxiously from the gravel path outside. How much bigger the door looked now—funny that—somehow. And here, on each side of him, was a door. And there were the stairs.

Well—which? The doors or the stairs? Silver below and jewellery above. That was the way of it, wasn't it? Why not both?

The cheese was operating.

He moved towards the staircase. Get the top done first and work downwards. Yes, that was it! But something worried him as he reached the staircase and put his soiled boot on the first worn stair, and he paused. What was worrying him?

He paused for five anxious seconds trying to discover what was worrying him. Not knowing was the worst worry of the lot! It wasn't just the silence, was it? No. He wanted silence. It wasn't the opposite, then—a noise? Had he heard a noise? He listened so hard that it hurt, even clenching his teeth with the idea that that would help. He heard nothing. The silence persisted. Not that. Was it the sort of heavy, suffocating atmosphere? No, again. Any one doing this kind of a job for the first time would feel a bit weak and wobbly. Even after half a pound of bolted cheddar.

Ah! Got it! He knew what it was. With a novice's inefficiency he was doing this the wrong way about. Get *downstairs* done first, and work *up*! What had worried him was that somebody might pop out of one of these doors while he was on the top floor, and then he'd be caught. Mug!

Of the two doors, one was ajar, and the other was closed, with the key in the lock. The door that was ajar was on his right. That would be the unshuttered front window. The door with the key was on his left. That would be the shuttered room. He had turned round from the stairs, and now had his back to them while studying the geography.

He went first to the room with the door ajar. After listening at the crack, he pushed the door wide and looked into a dining-room. In his hurry to get to the sideboard he tripped, caught hold of a chair and went over with it. The sound of the fall was thunderous. He felt sure it could be heard for miles around. But it produced no disastrous results, so he picked himself up, sucked a scraped knuckle, and completed the interrupted journey to the sideboard.

The sideboard drawers yielded a small harvest. He left the room with a dozen silver spoons and forks added to his normal meagre weight.

Was this enough? Yes. That tumble had shaken him, and the fog-horn had started up again—he could just hear it moaning its two mournful notes in the distance—and the heavy suffocating quality of the atmosphere seemed to be increasing. Yes, quite enough. He had filled his stomach well and his pockets modestly, and this kind of thing wasn't really in his line.

But as he looked at the door with the key, the itch of curiosity got hold of him, and he found himself moving towards it. That shuttered room—he'd have to take just a peep. It was the shutters that had first drawn his attention to the house. There might be something interesting behind them, and he was no longer worried by the question of an occupant. If there had been any one in the room, or the house, the noise of that fall in the dining-room would have brought them along!

Maybe he'd find an ornament or two to add to the forks and spoons.

He turned the handle. The door did not open. Locked. He turned the key. Now the door opened.

He had expected darkness. He looked into a blaze of electric light…

Ted Lyte never remembered leaving that house. The next thing he remembered was being out of it; and, as if he had not been given horror enough, he woke into a fresh nightmare. As he sped to the gate that still swung and groaned on its rusty hinges he heard footsteps speeding after him.

The shock of this produced a second period of oblivion, and once again he swooned mentally, although his legs kept on running. Had there been any spectators of this unique race, they might have imagined they were witnessing a new form of paper-chase, in which the trail was spoons and forks instead of paper. Ted's pockets were plentifully supplied with holes, and in the violence of his flight he shed much ballast. But there were no spectators on that lonely lane. For half a mile, pursued and pursuer had the road to themselves.

During the first part of the race Ted looked like winning. His velocity was volcanic, which was not surprising, since he imagined he was being pursued by Death itself. Then his pursuer gained ground, and gradually the gap between them shortened. It was the sound of the footsteps close behind him that finally brought him to and inspired his last frenzied spurt. He spurted into the widespread arms of a new enemy, who loomed abruptly ahead. He found himself flattened against a massive chest. His pursuer, shooting into his back, completed the sandwich.

"What's all this?" demanded the owner of the massive chest.

The speaker was a constable. Ted's luck was dead out.

"A spoon collector, I imagine," panted the pursuer. "I chased him when I saw him leaving a house in rather a hurry."

"'Urry? My Gawd!" choked Ted.

"Perhaps hurry is not the right word," admitted the pursuer. "He left the house as if he had been fired out of it from a cannon."

"Oh, did he?" said the constable. "What house?"

"Some way back along the road. I just came off my boat in time for the fun—hey! Watch him!"

For the victim had begun to screech with laughter. That word "fun" had crashed into his solar plexus.

CHAPTER II

Boredom Ends in Benwick

"DULL TIMES, SERGEANT," YAWNED DETECTIVE-INSPECTOR Kendall. "Damn dull times."

"That's how I like 'em, sir." answered Sergeant Wade.

"Yes, theoretically that's how we all ought to like 'em," agreed Kendall; "but it doesn't make for efficiency. How can I teach you your job when nothing happens?"

The sergeant rubbed his large nose. Personally, he thought he had had enough teaching during the past week to last him a year, and he was looking forward to the visiting inspector's departure. This gingering-up process didn't appeal to him at all.

"There was a fire on Tooseday," he murmured.

"Which was out before the engine got to it," retorted Kendall. "Anyway, that wasn't your funeral."

"Well, I expeck something'll happen as soon as you go."

"Oh, inevitably. The moment I turn my back Benwick will burst into crime! Meanwhile, what's that?"

He shoved a paper on which he had been doodling towards the edge of the desk, and the sergeant approached rather gingerly.

"Elephant," the sergeant guessed.

"An elephant has a trunk," replied the inspector. "Try again."

"Hippo."

"No, it's an elephant. There's its trunk. When you've formed an opinion backed by conclusive evidence, Wade, stick to it." His eyes suddenly narrowed as they travelled beyond Wade to the window. "Hallo—something happening at last?"

The sergeant did not turn at once. He thought this might be another trick, and he was still feeling a little hurt over the last one. But when sounds entered the passage he swung round and was just in time to share, with his superior, a strange sight.

A constable was carrying a small ragged man in his arms. The ragged man wore a vacuous expression, and was emitting sounds to match his face. Behind them was a light-haired young man with blue eyes and brown hair, wearing an open flannel shirt, grey shorts, no socks, and tennis shoes.

"What's the trouble?" exclaimed the sergeant. "Drunk?"

"Dotty, more like," answered the constable, depositing his burden in a chair. "Seems to have gone off his nut."

"Oh! Where did you pick him up?"

"He near bowled me over before I picked him up. This fellow was chasing him."

He jerked his head towards the young man in shorts and then produced a couple of spoons from his pocket with a significant wink.

"Ah, I see," nodded the sergeant. "Making himself at home with other people's property. Know where he got 'em?"

The young man in shorts stepped forward.

"I think this is where I come in," he said. "No, they're not my spoons. I'm just off my boat—it's in Havenford Creek—and I was about to ask my way at a house when our spoon-collector bounced out of it."

He had begun his explanation to the sergeant, but found himself finishing it to the inspector. The inspector, however, did not appear to be paying any attention to him. He was studying the strange crumpled creature in the chair. Ted Lyte's uncouth noises had ceased; he had passed into a stupor.

"That chap's had a fright," said Kendall.

"He met a policeman," explained the sergeant, a little too kindly.

"He's met more than a policeman," replied Kendall. "Hasn't anybody got anything out of him?"

"Not yet, we haven't, sir," answered the constable. "When we questioned him he jest—well—laughed."

"We did get one 'My Gawd' out of him," added the young man, "and I am inclined to agree with the inspector that there was more in his emotion than met the eye."

Now Kendall turned to the speaker and, after a swift scrutiny, asked:

"You're off a boat, you say?"

"Auxiliary yacht. *Spray*."

"Yours?"

"All of it."

"May I have your name?"

"Thomas Hazeldean."

"Thank you, Mr. Hazeldean. I'm Inspector Kendall. About this house. Where is it?"

The constable butted in: "From what he says, sir, it must be a house called Haven House; there's no other near it."

Kendall lifted the receiver of the desk telephone and called sharply, "Get me Haven House. Double quick!" Then, with the receiver still at his ear, he addressed Ted Lyte. "Ready to talk?" he inquired. "This is only a police station—our time's yours."

Neither the question nor the sarcasm produced any result.

"Who lives at Haven House?" asked Kendall.

"Man named Fenner," responded Sergeant Wade, feeling he had been left out a little too long. "With his niece."

"In residence now?"

"Ah, that I can't say, sir."

"They was two days ago," said the constable. "I know, because I see Miss Fenner in the butcher's."

The telephone operator's voice sounded in Kendall's ear.

"No reply," it called. "Their receiver's still off."

"Still?" queried Kendall.

"It's been off since yesterday."

"Oh, has it? You've tried the howler?"

"There's no response."

"What made you try it? Someone trying to get through?"

"Yes."

"When was that?"

"I'll find out." Then, after a short pause: "Yesterday afternoon."

"Do you know the time?"

"Between four-thirty and five."

"Was it a local call?"

"No, a London call."

"Between half-past four and five on Friday—yesterday—someone tried to phone Haven House from London, but the receiver was off, so they couldn't get through. You put on the howler, and no notice was taken of it. Is all that correct?"

"Quite correct."

"Know what part of London?"

"I can find out."

"Do. Find out all you can about that call, and keep the information by you in case I want it. Maybe I won't. Have you put the howler on since?"

"Twice."

"When?"

"Once last night and once this morning."

"Without result, of course?"

"Nothing at all."

"Right. Get me Dr. Saunders. Five-nine. Then try the howler again. If they answer, connect up at once and put them through to me the moment I'm finished with my next call. Otherwise, don't worry me till I worry you. Right."

While waiting, he caught the sergeant's expression and smiled. He guessed what the sergeant was thinking. The sergeant was thinking: "Showing off before an audience!" It didn't worry the inspector in the least.

"I hope that boat of yours isn't in a hurry, Mr. Hazeldean," he said.

"It's got all the time you want," answered the yachtsman. "I wouldn't miss this for a farm."

"Something to write home about, eh?"

"Well—you seem to think so."

"It was you who first suggested, Mr. Hazeldean, that there was more in this than met the eye," Kendall reminded him, "and since then we've got a receiver that's been left off, and the complete collapse of the only person here who might tell us something. Do stop prodding him, constable—that really won't help. Are we keeping anybody waiting, Mr. Hazeldean, besides yourself?"

"Only my crew," replied Hazeldean.

"A big one?"

"A big one and a small one. You don't lose any time, do you, inspector? You're finding out all about me. I like your methods."

"Then perhaps you'll mention them in that letter home," said Kendall dryly. "Ah!... Dr. Saunders?"

"Speaking," came the voice over the telephone.

"This is Kendall, police station. Can you come along right now?"

"Well, in about ten minutes."

"I'd rather you made it five."

"I dare say you would, but my car's out of commission."

"We'll send ours." The sergeant vanished from the room. He was learning. "You can walk to meet it, if you like," added Kendall. "It's a nice morning."

"What's the trouble?" inquired the doctor.

"I haven't any idea," answered Kendall, and replaced the receiver.

Then he rose from his chair and walked over to the prisoner.

Ted saw him coming through a mist. Since the original moment of horror he had passed through a succession of nightmares and a succession of mists, till at last life had become so unbearable that he had tried to assist nature and wipe himself out. That unbelievable moment, the chase to which the moment had given an added terror, the policeman, the laughter (was it his own?), and now the police station—what was there in existence worth holding on to? So he held on to nothing, and let his mind totter.

But this new policeman standing before him had a disturbing and menacing solidarity. He was like a doctor, bringing a dying patient back to pain. As the mist began clearing, Ted closed his eyes, substituting his lids for the fog. He opened them, however, when the new policeman said quietly:

"So it isn't only theft—it's murder, too, eh?"

For a few moments Ted stared into Inspector Kendall's eyes, held by their steadiness. Then, the words drawn from him, he whispered:

"I didn't do it."

"Do what?" asked Kendall.

The ragged man began to cry.

"'Ow could I?" he whimpered. "Orl that lot?"

And then a too-rapidly-filled stomach and a too-violently-shocked mind produced their delayed result, and he was sick.

CHAPTER III

Horror for Four

"HM! PASSED OUT," SAID THE DOCTOR. "YOU WON'T GET anything more from *him* for ten minutes!"

"We can't wait ten minutes," answered Kendall; "and we've already got quite enough from him to go on with. Stand by him, constable. Take down his statement when he comes back to earth, and see he doesn't give you the slip. A cup of tea may help the situation. Get through to Millingham, and tell 'em to send half a dozen men to Haven House at once. Maybe I'll just turn 'em back when they arrive, but it's pretty scenery. Now, then, doctor! Come along, sergeant!" He turned to the yachtsman. "And what about you?"

"You know my views," replied the yachtsman. "I'd weep if you left me out."

"I see. You want a prize for running?"

"I think I deserve it."

"You like this sort of thing?"

"It's my bread-and-butter."

The inspector shot him a swift glance. They walked as they talked.

"That's bad news," remarked Kendall. "I had a journalist trying to beat me on my last job."

"Yes. Bultin," murmured Hazeldean.

"Oh! You know that?"

"You mentioned your name. There are plenty of Kendalls in the world, but I remember one who did pretty good work recently at Bragley Court, in the case of the Thirteen Guests. What I liked about him was that he didn't play the violin, or have a wooden leg, or anything of that sort. He just got on with it."

"And there's another point you may remember, if you followed the case closely," said Kendall, with a dry smile. "He didn't give away any presents in exchange for compliments. Are you as bad as Bultin?"

"Not nearly," Hazeldean smiled back as they got into the waiting car. "But I'm bad."

The car darted forward. In three minutes it had shed the little town of Benwick and reached the spot where Ted Lyte had toppled into the arms of a policeman. In another three, a narrow, twisting lane had brought the party of four to the old gate swaying on its worn hinges. "Don't drive in!" ordered Kendall. Sergeant Wade, who was driving, pulled up sharply. The four men jumped out.

"Steady—just a moment!" came Kendall's next order.

He wanted the moment in order to register his first impression. Once this invasion began, fresh footprints would be on the rough, untidy gravel, and new incidents would mingle with old ones, confusing clues. Those clues had already been threatened by two intruders who—apparently—had no connection with the main object of the present visit. A silver fork, gleaming incongruously from the gravel, was the first evidence of this.

Swinging gate. Wanted oiling. Letter "O" almost rubbed out from words "Haven House" on gate. Gravel circling round grass plot. Gravel untidy. Grass plot ditto. Silver fork on right side of gravel. Disturbed spot near silver fork. Somebody tumbled? Small damaged bush near disturbed gravel. Somebody tumbled. Right lower window shuttered. Front door open...

"Which way did you come?" Kendall asked Hazeldean.

"Through a wood at the back," answered Hazeldean. "I was on that side lawn when I spotted my man—"

"Who was coming out of the house?"

"Well, that was an obvious deduction. Actually, he'd just reached this gate."

"Right! Come along! Keep to the left and stick to the edge—and when we get in, don't touch anything."

"Hey! What's that?" jerked the sergeant.

Something was happening in the house. As they darted towards it, an unearthly noise issued from the hall, and the sergeant admitted afterwards that it "fair went up his spine." The sound grew venomously. It was like a hive of bees that had gone mad. There seemed no rhyme or reason in it, unless it had been designed as a macabre overture to what was to follow. Even Hazeldean, whose nerves were exceptionally good, felt his heart accelerating, while the doctor's eyes became two little startled pools.

But Kendall smiled with ironic grimness as he dashed into the hall. He made for a small table on which was a telephone with the receiver off. Seizing the receiver, he bawled into it: "All right, all right—police speaking—stop that row!" He replaced the receiver, and the "howler" died away.

Then he swung round to a wide-open door. He was the first to look into the room and to see what Ted Lyte had seen. The others, their eyes on him, watched him grow rigid.

"My God!" he murmured.

"What—is it?" asked the sergeant.

"Come and see," answered Kendall. "Some work for you, doctor. Not that you can…"

They joined him in the doorway. The drawing-room they stared into might have been a morgue. Seven dead people—the doctor knew they were dead before he examined them—were in that shuttered chamber, revealed with a cruel starkness by the unnatural artificial light. Six of the people were men and one was a woman.

The nearest figure was on its face, head towards the door, and right arm extended. It was so close that the fingers almost touched Kendall's foot. A tall figure, with untidy dark brown hair. Across its legs, like the top part of a capital T, was a shorter man. His hair was black, and also untidy. Near the shutters of the front window were two men who looked something like sailors. The impression was conveyed by their coarse hands—one had tattoo marks on the back—and their jerseys. Probably the jerseys had been blue once, but now they were black with grime and age. Against the other shuttered window—the french window in the wall opposite the door—was an old, grey-haired man. He had a bald spot on top, and that also was grey. The sixth man was on a couch. His mouth was open, and one leg dangled. He might have been asleep, but for the grim implication of his silent companions. He looked the youngest of the company, though like the rest he was unshaven.

The woman was in a chair, her head resting against a blue cushion. It would have been easy at first glance to mistake her sex, for she was wearing a man's clothing—jersey, trousers and heavy boots—while her features, framed in short dark hair, were coarsened by exposure. She might have been attractive once. She was not attractive now. Her unseeing eyes were open…

Doctor Saunders ran forward.

"Be very careful, please," said Kendall, quietly. "I'll want photographs."

The doctor nodded as he bent over the first victim.

"Go over the house, sergeant, every inch of it," continued Kendall, "and report anything important you find the instant you find it."

The sergeant vanished with alacrity. Kendall turned to Hazeldean.

"Well, you're getting your scoop," he remarked. "Come round the room with me, but don't touch."

"Wouldn't I be more useful if I finished this floor while the sergeant does the top?" suggested Hazeldean.

"If you want to be useful, of course you would," answered Kendall. "Carry on."

The doctor, working rapidly, looked up as Hazeldean left the room after the sergeant.

"Stone dead," said the doctor.

"You're telling me," replied Kendall. "What I want to know is how he died."

The doctor continued with his examination, with a gloomy lack of confidence.

"Not going to be so easy, eh?" asked Kendall.

"We've both got nuts to crack," grunted the doctor.

"You're right. What's that on the back of his head?"

"An old scar. That didn't do it—though, from the look of it, it's a wonder it didn't do it at the time."

"How long ago?"

"Can't say."

"What can you say?"

"At the moment, Kendall, about as much as you."

"Which is nothing," smiled Kendall grimly. He gazed around. "This has Madame Tussaud's beaten. I expect they'd like it for their Chamber of Horrors. Can you see to-morrow's headlines?"

"Yes—I suppose our young friend is working them out now," replied the doctor.

"Well, it's his job, and you and I are doing ours."

"Ours are more useful!"

"That's merely our opinion. Something's in your mind. Let's have it."

Doctor Saunders glanced towards the door.

"Do you think *he* may have had anything to do with this?" he asked, lowering his voice.

"He may have," answered Kendall. "So may you and I. I once arrested a coroner just after he'd adjourned the inquest." He sniffed. "Get anything?"

The doctor sniffed.

"Not more than I expect."

"Can you say the same about their complexions?"

The doctor raised his eyes and stared round the room. He became unprofessionally human for a moment.

"I think we deserve medals for coolness," he said.

"It's our business to be cool," responded Kendall. "This isn't the first time you and I have seen death."

"I've never seen seven in a bunch like this!"

"No, and to my thinking seven's easier to stand than one. You can sympathise with one. Seven beats you—like the little boy in the Guitry film who lost all his family at once and didn't know which member to grieve for. I'm still waiting to hear what you've got to say about their complexions."

"And I'm still waiting to have something to say," retorted the doctor.

"Well, how's this, to go on with? When you've found what killed one, you'll have found what killed the lot… Hallo!"

He darted towards the fireplace and stooped. Taking a handkerchief from his pocket, he used it while picking up a small revolver to preserve fingerprints. With the same care he opened the weapon, examined the barrel, and closed it. Then he replaced the revolver on the carpet in the exact position in which he had found it.

"That didn't kill them," said the doctor, now shifting to the second body lying across the legs of the first.

"No. But what did it kill?" answered Kendall. "One chamber's empty." He added: "And who emptied it? We'll have to take seven fingerprints."

On the point of turning, he suddenly fixed his eyes on the mantelpiece. In the centre, conspicuously separated from the nearest ornaments, was a slender silver vase, designed for a small spray of flowers or a single bloom. There were no flowers in the vase now. Instead, incongruously supported on the top, was an old cricket ball. Like the jerseys of the seamen, it had lost all its original colour. It was green-yellow with age.

"Why's that there?" murmured Kendall.

He drew closer to it and examined not only the vase and the ball, but the spot where they stood. He noticed four little marks on the mantelpiece, two on each side of the vase. His eyes travelled along the mantelpiece to a clock at one end.

"Doctor, this mantelpiece is very interesting," said Kendall.

Saunders did not answer. He was moving to another body.

"Here is a clock with four legs," went on Kendall, "that has been moved from a perfectly good spot in the middle of the mantelpiece—its usual spot—thc lcg-marks arc therc—to make room for a ridiculous vase bearing a prehistoric cricket ball. The clock isn't going, but you don't put clocks in a corner for that."

"Here's something more interesting," replied Saunders. He was by the grey-haired man near the french window. "These shutters aren't merely bolted—they're nailed."

"Yes, I've already noticed that," nodded the inspector. "They're nailed at both windows." His eyes were busy all the while he talked. "But that doesn't undermine the importance of my cricket ball. I'd like to know its story."

"I'd rather know why the shutters were nailed up. The door wasn't locked."

"Not when we came in; but don't forget we weren't the first. That scamp at the station's going to tell us something presently." He moved to the doctor, who was now kneeling by the old man. "This poor chap looks a cut above the others, though his clothes aren't much better. Gosh, doctor—these people have been through something!"

"Through hell."

"But—before this, too! Don't you agree?"

"Yes, undoubtedly. Emaciated, most of them. This chap's condition is terrible."

"And plenty of will-power to endure it, I should say. Interesting face. I imagine we'll find that—hallo, there's something in his hand!"

He knelt down by the doctor and gently opened the fingers. The stump of an old red pencil rolled on to the floor. He picked it up and then stared again at the closed eyes of the man who had held on to the pencil while he died.

"My God, Saunders," muttered Kendall, "I'm going to find out who's done all this! If there's any after-life, this fellow's watching us!"

"There's someone else who's watching us, in a chair," murmured the doctor unhappily. "I'll go to her next." But before he moved away a look of despair entered his face. "I suppose you know, Kendall, I'm not getting anywhere?"

"No?"

"All I can tell you is that their hearts have stopped."

"Can you tell me how long ago they stopped?"

"I can only make a guess at that—so far. You see, *rigor mortis* varies, according to the cause of death, so if you don't know the cause of death, you don't know what to expect. We've no *rigor mortis* here. That gives us a range of from half an hour to twenty or thirty hours. You want something closer than that to work upon."

Kendall glanced at his watch. It was six minutes to eleven.

"Yes, I certainly want something closer than that," he said, "and I'm sure when you've finished here you can give it to me. There are other signs, aren't there, to an experienced doctor's eye—?"

"Well, yes, of course—"

"Have a guess. You'll be expected to, you know!"

The doctor studied the old man intently, then made a quick tour of the other bodies.

"I won't stake my reputation on it," he announced, at the end; "but—at a guess—I should say that death occurred not less than six hours ago or more than sixteen." He threw up his hands suddenly. "And that is assuming that they all died at about the same time."

"There's nothing definite to indicate that there was any great difference of time?" asked Kendall.

"No, no. Nothing."

"Then that will do, to go on with. We guess they were dead by five o'clock this morning, and alive at seven o'clock last night. I'll carry on with that, and maybe we can improve upon it later… Ah, sergeant!" He turned as his subordinate came into the room. "Any luck?"

"Not much, sir," replied the sergeant. "Nobody upstairs—dead or alive."

"I thought you were dead yourself, you've been such a time!"

"Well, sir, I made a job of it. Looked in every room *and* the cupboards."

He had also looked under the beds, but he did not mention that. He felt a little hurt at the inspector's attitude.

"You said, 'Not much luck,'" commented Kendall. "It doesn't sound as if you had any."

"One of the bedrooms was a bit untidy."

"Form any conclusion?"

"Well, sir, someone might have left it in a hurry. There's a pair of shoes—lady's—in the middle of the floor, like they was kicked off and no time to put 'em away."

"Anything else?"

"A dress half off a chair, like it was thrown there quick and they hadn't stopped to fix it."

"That the lot?"

"Barring no brush and comb on the dressing-table, like they'd been packed."

The sergeant thought this *piece de resistance* was a particularly smart bit of observation, and was disappointed that the inspector's face did not register admiration. However, he'd been in the force long enough to know that praise from a superior was rarer than currants in a bun.

"I'll go up in a minute," said Kendall. "Where's Hazeldean?"

"Adsum," came Hazeldean's voice as he appeared behind the sergeant; "and I've got something for you."

"What?"

"In the dining-room. Can you come and see?"

As Kendall followed him across the hall, he went on, half-apologetically:

"I ought to have found this before, but I explored the kitchen quarters first. Someone's got in through a back window; but that was probably our spoon-thief. He's left a lot of cheese crumbs. Here we are. This door was ajar."

Entering the dining-room, the inspector glanced swiftly around, and his eye rested on the overturned chair.

"Yes, but that's not what I mean," said Hazeldean. "That picture on the opposite wall. Damn' shame to treat a charming child like that."

The charming child was a girl of about eleven, painted in oils. She had soft brown hair and demure brown eyes, but there was a glint of hidden mischief in the eyes which the artist had effectively caught. The dress was white, with a blue belt, but there was something on the dress that the artist had not put there. A little hole.

"So *that's* where the bullet went," murmured Kendall, frowning. "Right through the heart!"

CHAPTER IV

Flaws in a Theory

THE DOCTOR'S VOICE RECALLED THEM TO THE DRAWING-ROOM.

"Here's your solution!" he exclaimed excitedly as they ran in. "I found this under him—what he was writing just before he pegged out. My God! Can you credit it?"

He held out a crumpled sheet of paper. On it was written, in bold capital letters:

WITH APOLOGIES

FROM

THE SUICIDE CLUB

Kendall stared at the half-dozen grim words, while the others looked at him. Then he stared round at the seven members of the suicide club. Then he stared at the paper again.

"No—I can't credit it," he said slowly. "This is in ink."

"Well, it was probably written before they committed suicide," retorted the doctor.

"And then he wanted to add something with the pencil?" queried Kendall. "Let's see if he did."

He turned the paper over. On the other side, in pencil, was:

"*Particulars at address* 59·16S 4·6E *G*."

The pencilled addition was not in bold capitals, but in ordinary, wobbly writing.

"And a thorough job they've made of it," commented the doctor. "I've looked at them all."

"Yes, and now it's my turn," answered Kendall.

He passed from one to the other, peering for several seconds into each face before going through the pockets. When he had finished he straightened himself and walked slowly round the room. As he passed the fireplace he paused to look up the chimney. Then he said:

"I'm going over the rest of the house and the grounds. I expect you've got some more to do yet, doctor. If you've finished by the time I have, and the others haven't turned up, meet me in the dining-room for a talk. Sergeant, stand by the doctor in case he wants anything. Come along, Mr. Hazeldean."

Hazeldean smiled as he left the room again with the inspector.

"Am I being useful," he inquired, "or is it just that you don't want me out of your sight?"

"Let's say a mixture of both," suggested Kendall. "I let you go once, and you found a bullet-hole I was searching for."

"Yes. And I didn't much care for the spot where I found it."

"Canvas doesn't feel pain."

"No. And some pictures deserve to be shot. Only this one didn't." The inspector gave him a sidelong glance. "Touché, inspector! That kid got me! What are you doing—looking for bloodstains on the stairs?"

"I'm looking for anything I can find, Mr. Hazeldean, but so far this seems to be a bloodless tragedy. What's your newspaper?"

"None in particular."

"I see. A free-lance."

"Yeah."

"Under nobody's orders but your own?"

"Are you sure that's going to make any difference?"

"We'll talk about that presently."

The top floor had four bedrooms and a bathroom, but only two of the bedrooms appeared to have been recently occupied. One of the two was obviously the room of the absent owner, Mr. Fenner, and the other, equally obviously, was that of the niece. It was the niece's room that had been the subject of Sergeant Wade's special report, and Kendall and Hazeldean agreed that its condition suggested a hurried departure. The two shoes—dark brown and rather worn, one of them on its side—were in the middle of the floor near the end of the bed, and the dress, a morning frock, made a little soft brown heap on the carpet beside a chair.

"Didn't I hear the sergeant say that dress was *on* the chair?" inquired Hazeldean.

"You did," answered Kendall. "The sergeant has been a naughty boy. Taken it up to examine it, and replaced it nearer the edge of the chair than where he found it."

"And it slipped down after he left?"

"You've got it."

"I suppose you're sure *you've* got it?" said Hazeldean. "Someone else may have taken it up to examine it."

"What? Since the sergeant left the room?" Kendall shook his head. "When you're surrounded with trouble there's no need to manufacture more! However." He walked to a wardrobe, opened it, and poked his nose into a row of dresses. "She uses violet scent."

"Quite smart," smiled Hazeldean.

"When you don't play the violin, or haven't got a wooden leg," Kendall smiled back, "smartness is all you've got to fall back on. Not that it needs much smartness to detect violet scent. Well, there seems nothing more up here. Let's get down."

"Will you answer a question?"

"Probably not."

"You don't believe in this suicide club, do you?"

"What makes you think that?"

"I can be smart, too."

"That's the trouble with you journalists. Sometimes you're too smart, and the smartness goes into the next edition before it's been properly digested. We're going to talk about the suicide club in the dining-room, but not till I've finished my preliminary investigations."

Inspector Kendall found nothing in the kitchen quarters beyond the evidence, already mentioned to him by Hazeldean, of Ted Lyte's visit; He examined the pantry window carefully, mentally cursing the little crook as he did so. Had the rascal's fingerprints obliterated any others? Yet he realised the debt of gratitude he owed the very man he was cursing. It was unlikely that Hazeldean would have entered by the back window after failing to get any response from the front-door bell, and but for the crook the tragedy inside Haven House would still have remained undiscovered, and Kendall would still have been yawning and doodling at the local police station.

He left the house by the back door, unbolting it to do so.

"That's the wood I came through," said Hazeldean behind him.

"And your boat's in the creek beyond?"

"Just inside the point."

"On holiday?"

"Combining work with it. Doing a yachting series. 'Yachting for Fools.' I'm a yacht maniac."

"And you came ashore to stretch your legs?"

"And to call at the post office for mail. Which, by the way, I've not done."

"Did you notice any dead animals as you came out of the wood?"

"No. Sorry."

"Cats?"

"Afraid not."

"There's one by that little gate."

"So there is." The yachtsman-journalist focused his eyes on the little black object, then turned to his companion curiously. "I take it you're not being just conversational?"

"I'm fond of conversation," answered Kendall, "but when I'm on a job I never indulge in it for its own sake. I once talked utter nonsense to a woman till she used the word 'knowledge' with a long 'o'. I'd heard that pronunciation over the telephone—and she's in prison now for attempted poisoning. You came round by the side lawn, didn't you?"

"Whew! Yes."

"We'll do the same."

They walked round slowly. Kendall paused at the french window to examine it, and when they came to the front of the house, went right across to the narrow path on the other side. He vanished along the path, returning abruptly at the sound of a car in the lane.

"I think, your reinforcements," said Hazeldean.

"About time, too," grunted Kendall. "Will you go into the house while I speak to them? I'll join you in the dining-room."

Hazeldean nodded and complied.

He found the dining-room empty, and while he waited he stared at the painting of the pretty little girl with the bullet through her heart. He wondered where she was, and whether the shoes in the bedroom upstairs belonged to her. Three rooms in this grim house had stories to tell, but walls lack tongues. What were the stories—and how did they all connect?

Figures moved outside the window. One came and stayed. The back of a constable made a sinister blot on the view. Footsteps sounded in the hall, and low voices. The incredible tragedy of seven dead people was being revealed to new eyes. Neither the footsteps nor the voices interfered with the brooding silence of the place. They seemed in a queer way to accentuate it, to develop it into a conscious thing… Hazeldean turned suddenly, as the doctor entered the room.

"Well, have you got your headline?" inquired Doctor Saunders rather acidly.

"I'm always open to suggestions," replied Hazeldean. "Have you one?"

"How about 'Mass Suicide'? That ought to draw the pennies."

"Yes, but the coroner's jury might not agree. I think I'll wait for the inquest."

They heard Kendall's voice in the hall. He was telephoning to the local station. A couple of minutes later he joined them, followed by Sergeant Wade and a portly inspector from Millingham.

"Inspector Black," Kendall introduced the latter, and then turned to the Millingham officer. "This is the Mr. Hazeldean I've mentioned."

Black stared at Hazeldean without much favour and then gazed round the room.

"Looks like a bit of a rough-house," he commented, when his eyes rested on the overturned chair.

"That's what I thought when I first came in here," answered Kendall, "but that chair was knocked over by our burglar."

"How do you know that?" exclaimed Hazeldean.

"Just learned it from the station," replied Kendall. "The fellow's begun to talk. It's that picture we're more interested in, Black. See it? I want you to tell me why seven people about to commit suicide in a stranger's house should begin by shooting a painting?"

On the point of answering, Black turned again to Hazeldean, and Kendall quickly interpreted his confrere's dubious expression.

"You needn't worry about him," said Kendall.

"Aren't you taking me very much for granted?" asked Hazeldean.

"Tell me if I'm wrong?" suggested Kendall.

"If you were wrong, I obviously wouldn't tell you."

"If I were wrong, you wouldn't indicate any flaw in my logic."

"Suppose I were subtle?"

"Suppose I am? Carry on, Black. This man may turn out a thundering nuisance before we're through, but meanwhile he may be useful to us, and we can take it he hasn't killed seven people. Besides," he added dryly, "haven't these seven people committed suicide?"

"You don't think so," retorted Black.

"But you do?"

"How do you get away from that written message?"

"Ever heard of a red herring?"

"Well—yes—there's always that possibility," admitted Black slowly. "Yes, certainly. Only somehow it doesn't seem quite logical—"

"Whereas it is perfectly logical," interrupted Kendall, "for seven people—emaciated, filthily clothed, ill assorted, and with nothing on any of them to identify any one of them—to walk through country lanes unseen—"

"How do you know they walked?"

"I'm guessing they didn't arrive in the Lord Mayor's coach."

"And how do you know they've not been seen?"

"We can check up on that, anyway. But, whether they were seen or not, and whether they arrived on roller-skates or stilts, they end their journey at a conveniently unoccupied house—"

"May I interrupt?" asked Hazeldean.

"I want you to interrupt," replied Kendall. "I'm making statements to annoy you into offering better ones."

"Well—since I've got to justify your hope that I may be useful—I think I've hit upon two flaws in your reasoning already."

"Number one?"

"If seven people set out to commit suicide, they wouldn't march with drums, flags and banners."

"You mean, they would try not to attract attention. Objection allowed. *If* they set out to commit suicide. Number two?"

"You used the phrase 'conveniently unoccupied house.' Plenty of houses are unoccupied."

"Probably a house-agent would corroborate you. Nevertheless, Mr. Hazeldean, this time it's objection overruled. *You* set out, as one of a party of seven, and march through a district of which you have no previous knowledge, and see whether *you* can find an unoccupied house so convenient that you can enter it—have you wondered, by the way, how they entered it?—and make use of it for wholesale self-destruction. Of course, your party may be lucky, but the odds are that you'll be wandering about all day and all night."

"All right, but why *shouldn't* they have had a previous knowledge of the district?" inquired Black, "and of the house itself, for that matter? There's nothing in their message to preclude it."

"I agree. That's one point I'm getting at," answered Kendall, "because to me it makes the whole suicide theory less feasible. Seven people calling on a person they know, to die in his house while he's out, eh? A queer sort of a joke! And, if there were any point in the joke, it should be self-evident without a message. Listen. I'm not putting the suicide theory out of court. There's some mighty queer story behind all this, and maybe, when we've unearthed it—as we're going to—suicide will fit the climax. But I'm not going to accept that theory until it's explained to me how they got into the house, why they nailed up the shutters, why they stuffed two weeks' papers up the chimney, how they destroyed themselves—that's your job, doctor, and it's going to mean Westminster Abbey or professional extinction for you!—who used the revolver, why he or she shot a picture in another room, where the Fenners are, why they left in a hurry, and how the devil—here's another little tit-bit I've just had from the station, Mr. Hazeldean—how the devil these seven people, before settling down to their final job, locked themselves in the drawing-room *with the key on the outside.*"

CHAPTER V

Miss Fenner's Time-Table

ABOUT AN HOUR AND A HALF LATER DETECTIVE-INSPECTOR Kendall walked slowly through the little wood at the back of Haven House—it was not the first time he had done so—crossed a small open space to the edge of a muddy cliff, paused for an instant to gaze at a trim auxiliary yacht in the creek mouth below, and then descended to it by a slippery, tortuous path. Tom Hazeldean saw him coming, and had rowed the dinghy to the rotting landing-stage by the time he arrived.

"Can I come on board?" asked Kendall.

"'Course," replied Hazeldean. "I've been expecting you. Do you like Bristol Cream?"

The inspector smiled. About to step into the dinghy, he stopped for a few moments to scrutinise a mooring-post.

"Have you used this?" he inquired.

"No," answered Hazeldean. "My man rowed me over this morning and then took the dinghy back."

"And came for you in the dinghy when you returned?"

"That's right. Same as I've done for you."

"I shouldn't say this landing-stage is used by many people, from the look of it," commented the inspector.

"One would hardly select it, if there was any choice," agreed Hazeldean.

"And there isn't any choice. Well, let's make for that sherry."

In three minutes they were on board the *Spray*. Their arrival was watched by the crew—an old man and a small boy—in respectful silence. The bottle of Bristol Cream was already on the long, narrow table of the saloon cabin when Kendall entered it.

"A good wine to fit a good boat," commented the inspector.

"The boat's even better than the wine," responded Hazeldean. "One day, when you want a holiday, I'll take you round the world in her."

"What can she do?"

"In the wind, all that's going. Under power, twenty. But I warn you not to get me on this subject, if you want to talk business. Help yourself, will you? And then give me the latest low-down."

"I'd like *your* low-down first," suggested Kendall, as he filled his glass. "What have you been doing with yourself since I let you off the lead?"

Hazeldean grinned.

"I've been a fairly good boy," he said. "Better anyway than Bultin would have been in my place, though I make no promise to keep it up. After you removed my dog-collar with a warning, I returned to the village, called at the post office for letters—there weren't any—inquired whether the Fenners of Haven House had left any forwarding address—"

"Oh, you did that?"

"It seemed a bright idea."

"But it drew a blank."

"I see you also had the bright idea! Then I telephoned my favourite editor, who is going to publish what I told him in the afternoon editions."

"And what did you tell him?" asked Kendall.

"This," replied Hazeldean. "Any complaints?"

He handed his guest a copy of the conversation. Kendall read it rapidly, then said:

"Thank you. That satisfies me. Did it satisfy your editor?"

"If he could have kissed me over the telephone, he'd have done so."

"I suppose you'll be handling the story for him?"

"He asked me to, but my terms were too high."

"May I know what they were?"

"A hundred pounds a word. As that was too stiff, I told him to send one of his own men along to carry on. He's doing it."

"What was your idea?"

"I thought you were good at guessing."

"You wanted a free hand?"

"That's it. If I get a scoop for publication, he shall have it before any one else; but I'm not going to be tied."

Kendall regarded his glass thoughtfully, then asked, "Aren't all journalists tied?"

"If they're inside men, certainly. Then they do what their editor tells them. But I'm an outside man."

"I see. Yes, of course. Have you any special reason for wanting a free hand in this particular case?"

"Inspector, I've told you a lot," responded Hazeldean, smiling, "and now I think it's your turn."

Kendall nodded.

"Right! I've been busy, too," he said. "You deserved your glimpse of the inside of Haven House, because you brought us the bad news and you haven't taken advantage of the situation; but you couldn't get in there now even with the incentive of a hundred pounds a word—"

"Couldn't I?" murmured Hazeldean.

"You can judge by the reception your brother journalists will receive when they turn up—and, incidentally, we've had one nosing round already. Ill winds blow fastest. He found constables at every gate and door, and they were disappointingly mum. Just the same, Mr. Hazeldean—"

"You can cut out the Mr., if you like."

"Thank you. Just the same, you needn't think your editor is going to get a monopoly. You can't keep seven dead bodies quiet—so to speak. This afternoon's placards will just shout. But there'll be more noise than information."

"Don't you want publicity?" asked Hazeldean.

"Not more than I've got to have," replied Kendall. "These next few hours are going to be damned important, and if I could have had six of 'em start of the press and the public I'd have been glad. Maybe it'll all work out the same in the end, only—" He gave a little shrug. "Well, when you're setting off on a chase, it helps to begin before the hare knows you're on the track."

"You're convinced this isn't a case of mass suicide, then?"

"I'm not convinced of anything, but I'm certainly not banking on suicide. Put it that way and draw your own conclusions. We've got a lot to do yet, both inside and outside the house. Photographs, fingerprints—" He paused. "We've found a key."

"What sort?"

"Latch-key. It was found under a little grating just outside the front door. As if it had been dropped. We had to prise the grating up to get it."

"Was it a latch-key to the house?"

"Are you going to phone my replies to your editor?"

"I haven't made any promises to my editor, and I'm not making any to you, so don't tell me anything that seems to you like a risk."

"You've two qualities that appeal to me, Hazeldean," said the inspector. "You're independent, and you're frank about it. I'm taking the risk. It was a latch-key to the house. Yale pattern, with a nice smooth portion where you hold it. I've taken a fingerprint. And I've found some more prints exactly like it inside."

"In the shuttered room?"

"No, though I'm getting plenty of prints from there, too. These were in the bedroom that had been left in a hurry."

"Miss Fenner's!"

"That is the assumption. You remember the sergeant making a big point of the fact that there were no brush and comb on the dressing-table, but there were several other things. A clothes-brush, a hand-mirror, and so forth. We found the similar prints on these."

"I—see," answered Hazeldean slowly. "And, of course, the inference is—"

"That Miss Fenner had the key, and either dropped it or hid it. Of course."

"Not a very clever place to hide a key, was it?"

"An idiotic place," agreed Kendall, "which suggests that, if she did hide it, and if she possesses average intelligence, she hid it in a great hurry caused by some urgency of the moment. Unless—yes—unless she believed the key would fall right out of sight, and was unable to get at it again on finding that it remained in view. I told you that we had to wrench the grating up."

"I can't see why she should hide the key," said Hazeldean.

"There's a great deal we can't see," returned Kendall. "Still, I incline myself to the theory that she dropped it. Some time between 8.30 and 9 last night." While Hazeldean stared at him he went on: "According to Dr. Saunders, our seven dead persons may have died round about that time."

"You're—you're not concluding—!" began Hazeldean.

"I'm not concluding anything," interrupted the inspector. "I'm not even concluding that the seven victims *did* die round about that time. I am merely implying that they could have. Unlike you, Hazeldean, I did not confine my inquiries about the Fenners to the post office. I also inquired at railway stations, police stations, and ports. I haven't been able to trace anything about Mr. Fenner—rather curious, that—but I have quite a lot of information regarding the niece. Some of it came from the world's oldest porter at Benwick."

"May I hear the information?" asked Hazeldean as Kendall paused. "It won't be passed on to my editor withour your permission."

"No—I am giving this to you on that understanding," answered Kendall. "We've already assumed that Miss Fenner left Haven House in a hurry. We can now assume that she was in a hurry to catch the 9.50 a.m. train yesterday morning for Liverpool Street—"

"But I thought you said—" interrupted Hazeldean.

"Wait a moment. She took that train, and travelled to London on a monthly ticket. After that we lose sight of her for a while, but we may note the facts that the 9.50 from Benwick reaches London at midday, and that the abortive phone call from London to Haven House—you remember about that—?"

"Yes," nodded Hazeldean, following the inspector's details intently. "The caller couldn't get on, because the receiver was off, and there was no response to the howler."

"You've got it exactly," answered Kendall. "Now add this. The call was made from a public call-box at Victoria Station at 4.42—that is, at eighteen minutes to five yesterday afternoon—and the caller was a woman with, to quote my informant's words, 'a pleasant, youngish voice.' Let us assume, just to see where it leads, that the owner of this voice was Miss Fenner. Let us also assume that a young woman answering Miss Fenner's description, who bought a third-class return ticket to Boulogne at Victoria some half-hour earlier, was Miss Fenner. Now, then. She leaves Benwick in a hurry, without troubling to tidy her room. My information is that she is normally quite tidy. She reaches Liverpool Street at midday. She vanishes till, roughly, a quarter-past four. Reappearing at Victoria, she buys a return ticket to Boulogne. Assumedly she intends to catch the 4.30 boat train. She does not do so, for at 4.42 she is telephoning back to her house. She gets no response. No one is at the house, or else someone is there who has decided not to answer telephone calls. The latter may be unlikely, but seven dead people are unlikely—"

"They weren't dead then," interposed Hazeldean.

"We do not believe they were dead then," corrected Kendall. "Having failed to speak to the person she wanted to speak to, Miss Fenner returns to Liverpool Street Station, catches the 5.57 train back to Benwick—where she is seen by the aforementioned ancient porter—"

"Whose eyesight mightn't be good."

"I admit that. This porter's evidence is not conclusive."

"Did she speak to him?"

"No. 'She went by me quick as a rabbit,' were his words. He could not even remember whether she carried a suitcase. The time was 8.16, so bad light was added to bad sight. Still, let me continue with these assumptions. Miss Fenner passes the old porter as quick as a rabbit and hastens—we assume—to Haven House. Our only evidence of this is the key; and, of course, that may have been dropped earlier. We know nothing more about her—nothing definite—until she is back at Benwick Station, buying another monthly ticket to London—the clerk has better sight than the porter—and leaping into the last train to town—the 9.12. She catches it by a matter of seconds. She is in London once more by 11.15."

"And that's all you know?" inquired Hazeldean.

"Not quite all," answered Kendall. "I made an obvious inquiry, and found that she slept at Liverpool Street Station Hotel. Next morning—this morning—she got up early and took the 9 o'clock boat train for Folkestone." Kendall glanced at the cabin clock. "Her passport was examined in Boulogne about forty minutes ago."

He got up from his chair.

"Well, I must be getting back," he said. "By the way, I don't suppose you've seen any suspicious characters or craft about here?"

Hazeldean shook his head.

"And you've nothing else to tell me?"

"Afraid not," said Hazeldean. "I expect your next informant will be Miss Fenner herself?"

"I'm hoping so. Only she's vanished again. She may be on the Paris train, but in that case, most likely she'd have booked right through. She's probably in Boulogne. The Fenners go there sometimes. Funny thing, though, nobody can tell me where they stay."

He held out his hand. As Hazeldean took it he inquired casually:

"What's this description that's being circulated?"

"Of the girl?" responded Kendall. "Only for official use, of course. Height about five foot five. Rather pale complexion. Very little make-up. Good figure. Pretty. Demure. Brown hair. Brown eyes. When last seen, wearing black coat and skirt, black shoes, white silk blouse and small black hat, and little green brooch at neck of blouse."

"The little girl in the picture had brown hair and eyes," commented Hazeldean.

"Same girl," said Kendall.

"But—from this description—with a different spirit."

Kendall nodded thoughtfully.

"Queer," he observed, "how life sometimes knocks the joy out of you."

CHAPTER VI

Trailers in Boulogne

After Hazeldean had rowed the inspector back to the landing-stage, he remained in the dinghy till his guest had climbed the precipitous path and vanished over the top towards the little wood leading to Haven House. It seemed impossible, in the peace and silence immediately around him, that a grimmer peace and silence lay only a little way off, concealing a tragedy of hidden origin. It seemed even more impossible that the tragedy could be linked with the child who had smiled out of the picture.

"No, no, *not* with that child," came the contending thought. "With the girl that child has grown into!"

Height about five foot five. Rather pale complexion. Very little make-up. Good figure. Pretty. Demure. Brown hair. Brown eyes. When last seen, wearing black coat and skirt, black shoes, white silk blouse and small black hat. Little green brooch at neck of blouse...

A fish jumped. He turned to watch the widening circle on the disturbed surface of the water, and as the rim touched and faded out against the landing-stage, an odd comparison entered his mind. The impulse of an unseen fish had caused this little disturbance. Emotion of a different kind, yet responding to the same basic principles, had occurred in the silent house beyond the wood, and its invisible circle had widened to the shores of Boulogne—and faded out.

He lit a cigarette. He visualised Inspector Kendall walking through the wood, his keen brain busy, his sharp eyes skinned for clues. Then he tried to visualise Dora Fenner and the spot in Boulogne that contained her at that moment—if she were still in Boulogne. The inspector believed that she was, and Hazeldean agreed with this belief. Was she near the wide bridge spanning the river? Was she climbing one of the narrow streets of steps in the fishermen's quarters? Was she walking, unconscious of trouble, in the green, flowered gardens beyond the Casino? Was she ascending the steep, wide road at the back of the town towards the ramparts?

"Ramparts," murmured Hazeldean. "Ramparts. Something about ramparts. What about ramparts?"

For a few seconds his thoughts puzzled him. Why had the ramparts entered them so vividly? He knew Boulogne well, but he had only once been on the ramparts which encircled the old town, hiding it from the new behind thirteenth-century walls. Why on earth...?

Then, in a sudden flash, the solution came to him.

The mind takes many photographs, but all are not immediately developed, and some, failing to meet the right circumstances, are never developed at all. Now, on the surface of the muddy water at which Hazeldean was moodily gazing, came the vision of a little mantelpiece, and on the mantelpiece a picture postcard. The picture was of La Porte des Dunes, showing a portion of the ramparts, and the mantelpiece was Dora Fenner's. He had noticed it subconsciously during his few moments in the bedroom with Inspector Kendall. The knowledge that its owner was in Boulogne now developed the latent memory and gave it significance.

Kendall had mentioned two of Hazeldean's qualities—frankness and independence—but this rather unusual young man possessed two more of which the inspector also had some inkling. One was a romantic disposition which he was apt to conceal beneath a mask of levity. He dreamed in secret, and the beckoning horizons of the sea fed his imagination. The second quality was impulsiveness. He was not impulsive in small matters; the lesser details of his life were dictated, as a rule, by a practical, well-ordered common sense; but periodically some compelling impulse caused him to throw the common sense overboard and to indulge in adventurous madness. His friends had called him mad when he had given up an excellent and lucrative position in a journalistic office. They had called him mad when he had spent most of an unexpected inheritance in an auxiliary ten-ton cruiser. They would certainly have called him mad now had they been aware of the impulse that caused him suddenly to toss away his half-smoked cigarette, swing the dinghy round and make for the *Spray* with rapid strokes.

"Full steam ahead, Bob!" he shouted before he reached the side.

"Ay, ay, sir," came the senior member of the crew's voice. "Where for? Mersea?"

"Boulogne," answered Hazeldean. "And we're going to do it in record time."

"There ain't much wind," commented Bob Blythe.

"Wind, be blowed," retorted Hazeldean. "We're using petrol."

Bob grimaced, then accepted the situation philosophically. He never liked petrol. It could get you about, true, but it was an insult to the sea, which had been designed under wind and should therefore have stuck to it. To the average map-reader, the land is full of interest and the sea is just a flat blue space, but to those who lived in boats—Bob had lived in boats all his seventy years, and he hoped his grandson would do the like—this flat blue space is a storehouse of interest; and Bob knew, for instance, that between Haven Creek and Margate Road he would be concerned with such places and locations as Maplin Sands, Oaze Deep, Shivering Sand, Kentish Flats, Shingles,

Tongues, Girdlers, Horses and Spits. All these had to be reckoned with, and petrol had a nasty habit of diminishing their importance. Still, there you were! Times moved, and boats with them; and Bob had to admit that, when choice existed, his captain preferred to move under seven hundred square feet of canvas.

By two o'clock Essex was receding into the haze, and the north Kent coast was becoming clearer. The morning mist had curled away, and conditions were perfect. By three the boat had curved round North Foreland and was heading south for the Channel, keeping inside the Goodwins. "She's goin'!" grinned Joe, the junior member of the crew.

"She's meant to," retorted the captain.

He kept her going till she reached Boulogne.

"More waitin'?" inquired Bob, as the *Spray* entered the harbour.

"Afraid so," answered Hazeldean. "But be ready to start off again the moment I return, if necessary."

"Ay, ay, sir. Where will it be next time? South Pole?"

The chance jest reverted to Hazeldean's mind later.

The late afternoon sun was burning on the cobbles when he found himself free to begin the next stage of his strange adventure. He stood for a few moments on the wide bridge over the River Liane, raising his eyes towards the hill that formed his objective. On that hill was the Haute-Ville, the original Boulogne, nestling within high walls like a bit of sunken history. Ghosts lurked there for those with vision to see such things: the ghosts of Godfrey de Bouillon and his crusaders; of English soldiers storming and capturing the terrified town; of Napoleon and his vast army, waiting for the moment that never came to invade England's shore; of an Unknown Warrior, who rested for one night before returning home to English soil. But Hazeldean saw none of these ghosts in his mind's eye. His ghosts were seven more recent spectres, disturbing a quiet spot to which they seemed to have no right…

"Shilling. Very pretty. Only one shilling."

He turned. A dark-skinned man was smiling at him, showing very white teeth. Over the man's arm were silks of many colours.

"No, thank you," answered Hazeldean.

"Very pretty," urged the man. "Take back to your lady."

"I haven't got a lady," replied Hazeldean.

"*Domage!*" smiled the man.

Hazeldean walked on. Something worried him, though it took him several seconds to discover what it was. Hadn't he seen this man before—near the quayside where he had landed? Then he rounded on himself. Even if he had seen the fellow before—though there were dozens of street vendors like him, intent on dazzling unwary trippers with colourful bargains—what did it matter?

Still, he continued on his way with senses alert, and when he had crossed the Quai Gambetta and entered the Rue Faidherbe, he stopped again suddenly and turned. The dark-skinned silk vendor was a few paces behind him.

"Come here!" he called.

"You change your mind?" responded the man, hurrying up. "I think you would!"

"And that's why you've stuck on my heels?" inquired Hazeldean.

"Stick on the heels," mused the street merchant. "Ah! To follow! Oui, m'sieur. I stick on the heels. Once, no buy. The second time, yes. The first time, a swindle. Yes, I hear that word quite much. The second, perhaps not. Perhaps a bargain. Perhaps you remember you could not buy so pretty silk in London for one shilling? *Voyez!* The yellow corn colour. Shilling. For the lady you do not yet meet!" He grinned, once more displaying his excellent teeth. "Shilling."

Hazeldean smiled back, and paid the shilling. The man whipped the corn-coloured square from his bundle, folded it deftly on a raised knee and handed it to his customer with an air of modest triumph.

"Good luck," he said.

"Meme to you," answered Hazeldean, pocketing the silk.

To reach the Haute-Ville he had to turn to the right, but instead he turned to the left. Wandering casually, he made his way back to the Quai Gambetta and began strolling in the direction of the Casino. Presently he took his cigarette-case from his pocket, fumbled purposely and allowed four cigarettes to escape on to the cobbles. "Curse!" he murmured as he stooped to pick the cigarettes up. Out of the corner of his eye he saw the silk merchant some thirty yards behind him. Even at that distance, and in that quick glance, he recognised the man, despite his resemblance to others of his breed. He had studied him carefully during their last encounter.

An empty taxi came by. He hailed it, called, *"Wimereux, si'l vous plait,"* and jumped in. The taxi developed a speed as though the devil were after it; but the devil was merely a French taxi-man's natural lust for pace.

They sped round the Casino and along the short, fashionable sea-front. Wimereux was four miles distant; but when they had gone a mile the fare changed his mind and shouted a new direction. After all, he explained, he did not want to go to Wimereux just yet. He had forgotten an appointment at La Porte des Dunes. The car swung round and made for the Haute-Ville.

A few minutes later they had re-crossed Boulogne by another route and had ascended the long gradient to the ramparts. There had been no sign of the silk merchant on the return journey. Alighting at a grey stone archway, Hazeldean quickly paid his fare, paused for a hasty, satisfactory glance around, and then slipped through the arch. He ran up the steps on the right of the arch. Reaching the quiet seclusion of the wall-top, he paused again and took a pleasant, deep breath. All around was the peace of sheltering leaves and green grass and ancient stones. He had not merely shaken off the silk merchant; he had shaken off the whole outside world.

"Why on earth was that plausible rascal following me?" he wondered. "And how the devil does he know anything about me?"

It was a small puzzle inside a big puzzle. He was convinced that to find the solution of the one would assist towards the solution of the other.

"On a sudden impulse," his mind ran on, "I decide to cross to Boulogne. No one knows but myself and my crew. I am on my way a few moments after the decision. I do not go ashore and talk about it. If I'd crossed as an ordinary passenger—by train and boat, or aeroplane—I could have been picked up during the journey. Though, even so, I'm bothered if I can see the reason… I wonder…"

A startling idea entered his mind. Seven dead strangers had been found in Haven House. Had they missed an eighth stranger, who was still alive? It seemed impossible. But, then, as Detective Kendall had himself pointed out, everything seemed impossible. Seven dead people. The suggestion of mass suicide. The old cricket ball on top of the silver vase. The shot picture. The dead cat… "Why am I thinking of the dead cat? That can't be important!"… And now this silk merchant…

"Oh, well," he concluded, "sufficient for the moment is the problem thereof, and the problem of this moment is to find a pretty girl of five foot five, with a pale complexion, a good figure, and demure brown eyes. Will she still be wearing that black coat and skirt and the small black hat and the white silk blouse? There was something else. Something else. Something important I've forgotten. Blow! What was it?"

He swore at himself for forgetting as he began his long walk round the sunken town. He did not usually forget things. Something else. Something else. Perhaps this wide, shaded, walled path, with its drop to reality on one side and its strange romance on the other, had an eradicating influence. Some of the buildings of the town climbed up close to the wall and had doors leading on to it. The ramparts were their garden. Something else—something else. Probably it did not matter. Hallo—the old stones have crumbled a bit at this corner... Now round into the next short, shady vista. Something else. Jolly, those trees. What a perfect seclusion, this mellow spot, for the end of one's days! And there's the house for it, too! If you weren't keeping your eyes skinned, you would hardly notice the house was there at all. Bit gloomy, though. Perhaps, after all... Something else. Blow! Something else...

Ah! Suddenly he got it! "Little green brooch at neck of blouse." Now what had made him think of that all at once?...

It was the brooch itself that had made him think of it. A thin streak of sunlight, slanting through a crack in leaves, turned it into a vivid green point, which shifted into shadow as the girl on the seat moved slightly to raise her head.

CHAPTER VII

On the Ramparts

THE EYES THAT RESTED MOMENTARILY ON HAZELDEAN'S FACE were both brown and demure, but the demureness dissolved into a tiny, vague frown as the girl lowered her head again to the book she was reading, for Hazeldean had not been able to camouflage his emotion, the intensity of which surprised him. It was the little green brooch that had primarily directed his attention to Dora Fenner, and every other detail of the official description seemed complete; yet he felt that he would have recognised her, even if there had been no description at all, as the girl into whom the child in the picture had grown. His reaction to each had the same queer, disturbing quality.

"Well—what do I do now?" he thought.

The girl, of course, gave him no assistance. If she were aware that the young man who had suddenly stopped by the parapet had not resumed his interrupted walk, but remained still looking at her, she gave no sign, saving perhaps in a slightly exaggerated absorption in what she was reading. Hazeldean's problem was not the unsavoury one of trying to pick a girl up, but of avoiding that unpleasant appearance in order to secure her confidence.

He decided on a bold opening. Approaching her till he was close enough for a low voice to carry—he felt her tightening as he drew nearer—he said:

"Good-evening, Miss Fenner."

She almost dropped her book. The brown eyes were on his again, bright with both astonishment and alarm. He discovered within himself an intense desire to dispel the latter, and dreaded the moment ahead when he would have to introduce a far greater alarm than any she could now be feeling.

"I'm quite harmless," he smiled.

"Who are you?" she asked. "I don't know you. Do I?"

"No."

"Then—how do you know me?"

"I've seen your picture." Her bewilderment grew. "I'll explain that presently, if you'll let me," he continued quickly. "But first I'm going to find out whether you *will* let me." He knew she would have to let him, but he wanted to establish an easy relationship before he spoke of serious matters, and he was banking on his own personality and the responsive spirit he had glimpsed beneath the paint of the portrait. It seemed impossible that this spirit could ever have evaporated completely into demureness, solemnity and suspicion. "My name's Tom Hazeldean. That won't mean anything to you. I'm a—writer"—he thought "journalist" might alarm her—"and an amateur yachtsman. As a matter of fact, I've just come across in my boat especially to see you. Yes, look astounded, by all means—I would, in your place—but please don't look alarmed. I'll tell you something at once, to get it over. If there's any trouble, you can count on me to help you all the way through it. Does that sound any good, to begin with?"

"Yes—of course," she answered. "Thank you very much. Only I don't know what you're talking about."

"That'll come in a few moments. What I want to know is, are we over the first fence?"

"Yes."

"You don't want me to walk round the ramparts while you think about it?"

She smiled faintly. "You needn't do that. It would take you half an hour. Yes, I—I think we're over the first fence. What's the second one? And what did you mean by—trouble?"

He took a deep breath. He felt he had started well, for without her complete confidence his assistance would be negligible. One thing he had already learned, although another man—Inspector Kendall, for instance—might have waited for confirmation before making up his mind. Dora Fenner knew nothing of the tragedy at Haven House.

"Do you trust me enough, on this very short acquaintance, to answer a few questions?" he asked.

"Yes—I think so," she replied.

"But you're not sure."

She considered her answer before she gave it.

"I'm as sure as one could be, in the circumstances." Suddenly she shot a question of her own. "You said you are a writer. Is that all?"

"I added yachtsman. You must see my boat some time."

"You know I didn't mean that."

"What did you mean?"

"Are you—I mean—yes, are you anything to do with the police?"

"What makes you ask that?"

"I don't know. It just came into my mind."

"Well, Miss Fenner, I'm not. I'm just exactly what I said—plus, I hope, a good friend."

"All right. Ask the questions. Of course, it may depend on what they are."

He realised that she was trying hard not to let her anxiety get the better of her, and although he was banking on her ignorance of the major tragedy, he was convinced that the anxiety had existed before this interview. He was convinced of this both from her attitude and from the time-table of her movements on the previous day, as reconstructed by Inspector Kendall.

"O.K. We'll begin. Is your uncle here with you?"

"Oh! You know about him, too?" she replied.

"I know you've got an uncle—Mr. Fenner."

"Do you mean, is he in Boulogne?"

"Yes."

"Yes, he's in Boulogne. But not here at this moment."

"Where is he at this moment? Do forgive me if my questions sound a bit blunt—"

"That's all right. I don't know where he is. He went out after lunch."

"But you expect him back soon?"

"Yes."

"And I suppose he came over here with you?"

She did not answer at once. He watched a frown dawn. The cheeks that lacked make-up became a little flushed.

"No, we didn't cross together," she said. "I don't suppose it matters why we didn't. It was just—well, rather a mix-up. He crossed yesterday on the 4.30 boat—I mean, the train leaves Victoria at that time—but I only came over this morning."

"I see," murmured Hazeldean. "Your uncle was in Boulogne all night, then?"

"Of course."

"And you're quite sure of that?"

"Why, yes. Madame Paula—she runs this pension where we're staying—she'll tell you so."

Hazeldean raised his eyes, and looked beyond the seat at the small grey-stone building that climbed up from the encircled town to lean its chin on an inner edge of the wall. A little door, in a dark porch, was ajar. For the first time he noticed the name "Pension Paula" over it.

"If this is going to be a long conversation, hadn't you better sit down?" suggested the girl.

"Thank you, that's a good idea," he nodded and sat beside her. For some indefinable reason, he did not like having that half-open door behind them.

"It's a pension, then, is it?"

"Yes."

"Are there many people staying there?"

"No, only my uncle and me."

"You and your uncle and Madame Paula?"

"She runs it. Oh, I said that. She and her husband."

"Oh, there's a Monsieur Paula?"

"I don't know why you're asking—"

"I'm sorry."

"No, I am. I forgot for a moment I was letting you." She gave him a quick nervous smile, in a pathetically obvious attempt to wipe out her doubts. "What was the last one? Oh, yes. Monsieur Paula." She smiled again, momentarily becoming the child in the picture—laughing away the ogre with a joke. "Actually, his name is Jones. He's a doctor, but Madame Jones sounds funny, I suppose, so she calls herself Madame Paula."

"And Dr. Jones completes the party?"

"Nearly. Do you want the rest?"

"Might as well—while we're at it."

"There's a girl, a sort of maid—Marie. And there's an old man who does odd jobs—Pierre. That makes six, and that's all. I'm doing my best, aren't I?"

"You're doing wonderfully," he replied. "Please go on as you've begun. Apart from your uncle, is everybody at home?"

"Not Dr. Jones," she answered. "I've not seen him at all yet—and I don't want to!" The next moment she looked astonished at herself and a little ashamed. "Please pretend I didn't say that! I—I don't know why I did."

"You didn't say it," Hazeldean assured her. "What you said was, 'Dr. Jones is terribly, terribly nice, and I can hardly wait for him to turn up.' By the way, Miss Fenner, I'd better tell you something else about myself. I've an awful habit of making jokes in the middle of serious matters. They just come and go, and they don't mean anything, excepting that I adore fun. Once I got caught in a terrible storm at sea. I thought it was all up with the *Spray*. That's my boat. And all up with me, too. I was puffing and blowing and half-naked, and all at once I thought how funny I must look. It gave me a good moment. I grinned—and I pulled through."

"I'll remember that," said Dora Fenner gravely. "I expect you meant me to."

"I did," he admitted, "though I don't really think you need the reminder. That picture I saw of you—the one in the dining-room"—he was steering the conversation to its next phase—"I rather fell for it. I hope you don't mind? You looked so full of fun yourself."

"That was painted a long time ago."

"Oh, not so very long. And I've a theory that we never really change. Only our circumstances."

"What's the next question?"

"May I know why you came to Boulogne?"

"We do sometimes."

"Always to Madame Paula's pension?"

"Yes."

"Then there was no special reason why you came this time—and why you left Haven House yesterday morning in rather a hurry, even though you only arrived here to-day?" She stared at him. "Yes, I know quite a lot," he went on, "but I wish you'd tell it to me. I've only got details, and what I want are reasons. For your sake, remember. You might even be able to give the reason for an old cricket ball on a silver vase—"

He stopped abruptly at her expression. Her book slipped to the ground.

"You even know—about that?" she gasped.

"Is it important?" he asked seriously.

"I—don't know!" she answered. Her voice was unsteady. "Please wait a moment. This is all so confusing."

"Of course it is. I'll wait as long as you like," he replied.

He got up from the seat and strolled across the grass to the parapet. He believed it might help her to sort out her feelings if he removed himself for a few seconds. Below the parapet was an almost sheer green slope that dropped to the ribbon of road encircling the wall. In the distance were the roofs of outer Boulogne and gleams of water, but as his eyes began to travel farther afield they suddenly returned to the road. A familiar figure had come into view round the curve.

He left the parapet abruptly and returned to the seat. "Can we finish our chat inside?" he asked. "I think it would be a good idea, if you could arrange it."

The figure in the road below was the omnipresent vendor of coloured silks.

CHAPTER VIII

In the Little Parlour

SHE LED HIM THROUGH A DARK GREEN DOORWAY FROM THE leafy dimness of the ramparts to the greater dimness of a hall. As she paused to peer for an instant towards a curtain at the back he had a sense that he had left pure air for an atmosphere less salutary, and a vision of that unnaturally tragic room a hundred miles away came to him suddenly with macabre vividness. What had this girl, standing momentarily in a strained position, to do with such horror? And why was her position strained? He was the one who should have caused her uneasiness, but he was convinced she felt far less easy about somebody beyond that curtain. In the dark silence of the hall he heard her heart beating.

Then she moved—away from the curtain. She turned into a narrow passage that ended in a staircase, a short one of only half a dozen steps. The top step led almost immediately to a small door.

"You'll have to stoop, or you'll bump your head," she said.

A moment later they were in a parlour, and the door had been quietly closed.

It was a low-ceilinged room, quaintly proportioned, and almost as dim as the passage. The one little window had diamond panes, and half its meagre area was screened outside by the branches of a tree. A quick glance told him that it looked out upon the ramparts. He saw one end of the seat.

"No one will disturb us here," murmured the girl. "Please sit down."

He took a chair near the window. She took another by a small table. In the little silence that followed, each seemed to be waiting for the other to begin. The atmosphere between them had subtly changed. It was as though the closer walls had focused the unnamed mysteries that separated them, demanding with painful insistence that the mysteries should now be shared.

"Well—you want me to tell you things," she exclaimed suddenly, with a nervous raising of her voice.

"Yes, and you want me to tell you things, too," he answered. "But first can we settle a few preliminaries?"

"What do you mean?"

"You said no one would disturb us. Would it be awkward for you if any one did?"

"I see. Yes. Well, wouldn't it? I'd have to explain you."

"And you wouldn't know how to, because you're waiting for the explanation yourself! Is there a map of Boulogne in this room? Guide-book? Anything of that sort?"

"Yes."

"Can I have it?"

"On the shelf at your elbow. A map."

"Thank you." He turned and drew it out. "Fine! I'm a tourist, and I asked you if you could direct me to the Cathedral of Notre Dame. 'Certainly,' you said. You said it so nicely that I went on: 'It was built by Bishop Haffreingue, wasn't it?' And you said, 'Yes, it was.' And as you still hadn't snubbed me, and I was all alone in a strange town, I got most frightfully bold, and I said, 'I don't suppose you could also tell me where La Beurrière is? I don't even know *what* it is, but I've been told I simply must go there.' 'That's the fishermen's quarter,' you laughed. 'Do you want to go anywhere else, too?' 'Lots of places,' I answered. 'Then I think you'd better come in and consult my map,' you said. It was frightfully kind of you. And I came in. And here I am. And here's the map." He opened it on his lap. "And now, please, while I'm studying all these confusing roads and names, tell me everything that happened yesterday, and after that I'll tell you why I want to know."

"There's one thing I want to know now," she replied after a short pause.

"What is it?"

"Why I'm trusting you like this?"

"But that's easy, Miss Fenner! You're trusting me because you know you jolly well can."

"Yes—I think that must be it. Well, where shall I begin? Perhaps it had better be over breakfast. Yesterday, you know. My uncle and I—" She hesitated, then went on, with a faint flush on her pale cheeks. "We almost had a row. It sounds silly. I mean, the subject of it. He wanted to come to Boulogne, and I didn't want to."

"Well, I suppose you had some reason," prompted Hazeldean.

"Yes, of course. But that may sound stupid to you, too. I—I didn't care for the people here." She had dropped her voice, and she glanced towards the door. "It was just that."

"And did you have any special reason for not caring for the people?"

"Do you want that, too?"

"Not if you don't want to tell me; but I think it would be wise."

"Yes, only—only I don't think I can. At least—no, that can't have anything to do with what you've come here about."

"Then we'll let it drop," said Hazeldean, "and I won't refer to it again unless we both think it necessary. May I ask this, though?

Did your uncle have any particular reason himself for coming to this pension? I mean, you could have gone to some other place, couldn't you?"

She shook her head.

"He'd never do that. We always come here."

"I see. Had you been here before, lately?"

"Not for about a month."

"And was it a sudden decision of your uncle's to come here this time?"

"Yes, quite sudden. I didn't know anything about it till he suddenly spoke of it over breakfast. It sort of—caught me on the wrong foot. I mightn't have made a fuss if there'd been longer to think about it. We've never had a quarrel before—I mean, a serious one. But, anyway, after breakfast I went back on myself... No, wait a moment. Something else happened first. The—cricket ball."

"Ah, the cricket ball," murmured Hazeldean, his interest tightening. "What about the cricket ball? Did your uncle hurl it at you in a rage?" She looked astonished. "Sorry, Miss Fenner," he smiled. "I was just trying to be funny. It's that bad habit."

She answered, rather unexpectedly, "No, it's a good habit—one ought to do it more." It was the little child speaking again—the child who had forgotten how to laugh. Something tugged at Hazeldean's heart. He wished he could have dissolved the ugly facts that had brought him to her, and taken her to a dance. "Where was I? No, my uncle didn't throw it. He didn't have it. Somebody else threw it. It came through a window... All this sounds ridiculous."

"Perhaps it is. Did it break the window?"

"No, it was open."

"Which window was it?"

"My bedroom window. I was making my bed."

"Doesn't the maid make your bed?"

"Why do you ask that?"

"You know as well as I do. I am trying to find out, very subtly, whether you keep a maid."

"You needn't be subtle," she responded. "We don't keep a maid."

"But a cook?"

"Not even a cook. I look after things. Not here in Boulogne, of course. Where was I?"

"Still at the cricket ball," he answered. "I hope you don't mind all my interruptions. The ball has just come through your open bedroom window—and, naturally, you immediately rush to the window and look out."

"No, I didn't."

"Why on earth not? That's what I'd have done."

"I dare say; but I'm not you. People don't always do the same things."

"That's true."

"Besides, I was startled—and then upset, too, from the row. I hate rows. I always feel I'm in the wrong. I mean, with everybody, whether I'm really in the wrong or not. I didn't used to. When my father was alive I remember I always thought I was in the right… I don't know why I'm saying all this. Where—oh, yes. Anyhow, what I did was to stare at the ball. It came right on the bed. A horrid old thing. It looked as though it had come up from the bottom of the sea! I don't know why it gave me such a shock—I mean, even apart from coming in suddenly like that—but it did. When I did go to the window—at last, you know—I couldn't see anybody. Whoever had thrown it had gone."

"Your window's at the back, isn't it?"

"Yes, how do you know?"

"That'll come presently. What did you do then?"

"I took the ball to Uncle John—to my uncle."

"And what did he do?"

The worry in her half-shadowed face, a worry that only retreated temporarily when he joked, became more definite.

"It—it was very queer," she said. "I mean, he seemed even more startled than I was. He looked at it for a few moments without saying anything. I got a funny feeling—oh, well, that wasn't anything—"

"Please tell me," he interposed. "I believe in funny feelings!"

"Well—this *is* silly—I felt as if he was looking at a ghost!"

"The ghost of a cricket ball," murmured Hazeldean. "Why not? That ball was dead enough to have one."

"You've seen it?"

"Yes." He responded quickly to a startled light in her eyes. "No, I didn't throw it! At present I know as little about it as you do—almost. Yes? And then?"

"He ran to the window."

"What room were you in then?"

"Oh, I see. I'm afraid I'm telling this very badly. We were in the drawing-room. That's where I took the ball to him. What's the matter?"

"Nothing. The drawing-room. You were using the drawing-room, then?"

"Yes. Why not?"

"Only that when people manage without servants they sometimes close a room up. You know—fasten the shutters and lock the door, and have one less room to look after. But you didn't do that."

She gave him a swift, shrewd glance before replying, "No."

"Well—Uncle John ran to the window. By the way, which one?"

"All these details are important, aren't they?"

"Tremendously. No, that's wrong. They just may be."

"I'll give you all I can. He went to both windows: first the window in the front, and then the window that opens on to the lawn at the side of the house."

"Did *he* see anybody?"

"He didn't say so."

"But you thought he did?"

"I didn't say that."

"No, I'm asking you to say it now."

"Well, I—"

She stopped dead, then rose quietly and walked to the door of the parlour.

"Careful!" he warned in a low voice.

The warning came too late. She seized the handle suddenly and flung the door open. Then she closed it almost as quickly and returned rather weakly to her chair.

He looked at her with sympathetic reproof.

"Miss Fenner," he said, "may we interrupt our story for a moment—for the sake of the end of it?"

"What do you mean?" she asked, but her voice was rather guilty, as though she half-guessed what was coming.

"What would you have said if you'd found somebody outside that door?" he inquired.

"I don't know," she admitted.

"Would that have been a bit awkward?"

"Yes, I see."

"It would have rather upset our neat little tale about the map, wouldn't it?"

"I suppose it would."

"When you're at sea—in a boat—and you think a storm's coming, you don't try to hurry it up. Not that you could; but no matter. You study the signs and concentrate on being prepared, in the best position, for the storm when it strikes you—if it does strike you. Get the idea?"

"Of course. But I'm not clever at this sort of thing."

"Nor am I, particularly, but the two of us will make a team. Now, then, back to the story. Uncle John didn't say he saw anybody, but you got the impression that he did. Is that right?"

"Yes."

"What gave you the impression?"

"I don't know. Yes, I do. It was his manner. It—seemed to alter. Only I really wasn't sure. You can't always remember just how your mind works—anyway, I can't—and his manner may have been just about the cricket ball. I mean, he'd been upset—well, worried—no, upset—before that. As I told you."

"Did you have another look out of any windows?"

"No."

"What did he do next?"

"He came back to me, and I asked him what was the matter. He looked awful. He's been overworking. I asked him if he felt ill. At first he said he did, and then he said he didn't, but he needed a change and a rest. 'That was why I suggested Boulogne,' he said. Of course, I said then that I'd go, though I did say it wouldn't be much of a change."

"And what did he say to that?"

"He said he agreed with me, and we'd probably only start at Boulogne. We might go on to Switzerland or the South of France afterwards. He seemed relieved and also excited. I really was worried about him, and I'd have done anything he'd asked then. I thought less about the cricket ball and more about him—and, after all," she added, "as he said himself, the ball had probably been hit by some boys in the road, and they'd scooted immediately afterwards." She raised her eyebrows at him. "You don't think that?"

"It's a possible theory," he answered.

"Only you don't think it. All right, your turn will come presently. Anyway, I don't see what road the ball could have come in any window from. Where was I? Oh, yes, his excitement. He got something like a boy himself—who was off on a holiday, and who couldn't wait—like I used to be—and told me I was to catch the next train to London. There's one at ten minutes to ten. He told me to catch that."

"Bit of a rush, wasn't it?"

"Awful. I wanted to take a later one, especially when he said he'd have to take a later one himself. But he said I could buy some things in London if we were going on a long trip, and he nearly bowled me over by giving me twenty pounds for clothes. I'd never had so much in my life!"

"And that made you agree?"

"I expect it was part of the reason. Yes, of course. I wanted some new things badly, but it was also because *he* seemed to want it so much. I couldn't bear the idea of another dispute. I think I'd have died. I hate trouble. Well, never mind about that. I know I'm silly. Anyhow, when he said he'd join me at Victoria for the 4.30 boat train, I rushed up to my room, changed, hurled a few things in a suitcase, and somehow or other I got the 9.50. When the train began to move I felt quite dizzy."

"I'm not surprised. What happened to the cricket ball?"

"I don't remember."

"I suppose he put it somewhere?"

"I didn't see where."

"Do you know what kept your uncle? I mean, why he didn't leave with you?"

"He said he had some business to do."

"I see. By the way, what is his business?"

Her brow puckered, and she looked at him a little helplessly.

"He never talks about his work to me," she answered. "It's—it's a sort of rule. But he told me one thing. He's writing a book, and has to do a lot of study for it."

"Do you know what the book's about? I'm sorry for being so abominably inquisitive."

"That's all right. I'm answering all your questions because I know there's a good reason, and that, of course, you won't pass on anything private that I tell you." He wished she had not said that. "I've no idea what the book is about, but I think it's something to do with some theory or other, or experiment. Does it matter, or shall I go on with what I was telling you?"

"Please go on," replied Hazeldean. "You have flopped into your train, and are getting your breath back."

"Yes. When I got to London I shopped—I don't suppose you have to know the things I bought?—and in the afternoon I went to Victoria Station. Yes, what is it?"

"I didn't say anything."

"No, but you nearly did. I could tell by your face. Do you want to know what time I reached Victoria? It was at about four."

"I was wondering about your passport. But, of course, if you visit Boulogne a good deal, you'd have one."

"Oh, I see. Yes, I've had one for some time. I didn't have to get it specially. Well, as my uncle wasn't there yet—I didn't expect he would be; I was half an hour early—I had a cup of tea, but afterwards he still wasn't there. I began to grow anxious. The 4.30 boat train is the last one of the day, you know, so if he missed that he was done. Of course, he'd told me he might miss it, and that I was to go on anyway, but I didn't want to travel by myself, and to come here alone, so just before the train started I jumped out—I'd taken my seat—well, of course I must have, or I couldn't have jumped out—and let the train go on without me." She broke off with a little self-conscious laugh. "It was silly of me."

"I don't think so," said Hazeldean.

"But you know—I've told you—he was on the train," she answered. "He caught it by a matter of seconds, and must have got into his compartment just before I got out of mine. It was rather funny, really. At least, it would have been if I'd known and not got in a panic."

"Box and Cox, eh? But why the panic?"

"I don't know. I get panicky too easily. I didn't used to. I had a feeling I can't explain that—but, of course, that was silly too." She gave him a quick glance, as though seeking corroboration. "Anyway, what I did was—after the train had gone and left me there—I looked about for him, and then—as you know, because you said you knew—I telephoned to the house. That is, tried to."

"About ten minutes after the train had gone?"

"Yes. I remember seeing the station clock. It was just twenty minutes to five."

"And what did you do when you found you couldn't get on?"

"At first I didn't know what to do."

"What did you think?"

"I supposed my uncle had left, and that the house was empty. There's no one else. We haven't a maid. Oh, I told you that. And, of course, that's just what it was."

"The train journey from Benwick to Liverpool Street takes—how long?—a couple of hours?"

"About that. A little over."

"And your uncle had to get from his house to Benwick station, and then from Liverpool Street to Victoria. Say, four hours for the whole journey, eh?"

"I suppose about that." They both paused to calculate. "No, not quite so much, if he made good connections."

"I agree. Then we'll say three and a half hours. Oh, by the way, what about a car? You know, to Benwick station?"

"We haven't one."

"Then he'd walk?"

"Yes. Unless he cycled. No, he'd hardly do that."

"Oh, you've got bicycles?"

"He has one."

"But it wouldn't take luggage—though I suppose, like you, he only had a suitcase?" He watched a frown develop. "I'm asking too many questions?"

"No, you're not," she replied, "but they'd have to seem funny before I knew the reason, wouldn't they?"

"They would, and you're very patient, Miss Fenner. You'll hear the reason presently. Three and a half hours, and he just caught the 4.30 train. So he must have been out of the house by about one—one at latest. And since one the house has been empty, as it was at twenty to five, when you phoned. Well, what did you do after that? You were just going to tell me."

"I did another silly thing."

"You can leave out the adjectives."

"No, it was idiotic. I looked up the trains back to Benwick, and found there was one just before six. I decided to go back."

"For once I agree with your adjective," smiled Hazeldean.

"What?"

"When you got no reply to your telephone call, you assumed that your uncle had gone and the house was empty. So it *was* idiotic to return—unless, of course, you had some other reason?"

She considered for a few moments, eyeing him rather guardedly. During the little silence he heard footsteps pass by the window. Well, there was nothing in that, he told himself. Plenty of people walked along the ramparts...

"What would *you* have done," she suddenly challenged, "if you'd been me?"

"Waited to see whether my uncle turned up," he replied.

"We know he didn't turn up—I mean, he already *had*!"

"Yes, we know *now*, but you didn't know *then*. For all you could say, he might have been on his way, and you might have passed each other—one coming, t'other going."

"I see. Yes, we might. But you've forgotten something. I mean, that feeling I had. The panicky feeling."

"The feeling you couldn't explain?"

"Yes."

"Did you think something had happened to your uncle?"

"No, though he'd certainly acted funnily in the morning."

"Did you think something might have happened at the house?"

Her expression grew startled.

"Why should I?" she demanded.

"Well, if you did, I expect you had a reason," he responded.

"I didn't think that," she said. "At least—no, I didn't. Not then." He noted the qualification. "If I had, I wouldn't have gone back, would I? I mean, so late, and alone."

"That's true. But I'm still waiting to hear why you *did* go back."

"If you must know, it was because, though I'd agreed to go to Boulogne, I still loathed the idea," she explained, in a tone that lacked self-confidence. "I—I think I was just closing my eyes—sort of—and jumping at any excuse not to go."

"Well, I can understand that," he nodded.

"No, can you?"

Her quick eagerness at his agreement was a pathetic symbol of her lonely mind.

"Of course. You told me you didn't care for the people here."

"Yes."

"And, you remember, I didn't press you for the reason. But I did say I'd return to the subject if we both thought it necessary. Well—what do you think now?"

Suddenly the reason came, in a rush of released emotion.

"Dr. Jones tries to make love to me—and Madame Paula frightens me!"

She turned scarlet.

"That sounds pretty wretched," answered Hazeldean quietly, after a little pause. "Naturally you didn't want to come to Boulogne. May I go on with this subject for a moment and ask if you've told your uncle?"

She hesitated, then nodded, half against her will.

"What does he say?"

"He—tells me I'm silly."

"That there's nothing in it?"

This time she did not reply. In the silence that followed he tried, without success, to connect this new personal tragedy with the original tragedy which had brought him to Boulogne. He felt certain there was a definite connection, but the link between the two remained hidden. He wondered whether Inspector Kendall would have approved of this interview, and the manner in which he was handling it. He also wondered what his editor would think of the story he could write up if he chose. But he found his centre changing. Neither the police nor journalism had any interest for him now. He was not sure that they ever had. It was the picture of Dora Fenner that had sent his boat skipping across the water, and now it was Dora Fenner herself, materialising out of two-dimensional canvas, who clinched his determination to see the matter through.

The girl's silence was eloquent. It told him that her uncle was not only aware of the situation, but that he approved of it. Deliberately Mr. Fenner brought his niece to the pension of a woman whose husband was behaving like a cad. There must be some compelling reason for this, and suddenly Hazeldean wondered what part Madame Paula had in that reason?

"Miss Fenner," he said, "I want to say something before we continue with your story. I've implied it before, but now I'm stating it quite definitely. I'm tremendously honoured that you are confiding all this to me—a stranger. If ever you need a real friend—if you need one now—you can count on me completely from this moment."

"I do need a friend," she answered unsteadily, "and—I don't know why—but somehow I seem to be counting on you."

"Then that's fixed!" he responded cheerfully. "And we'll get on. You caught that six o'clock train back to Benwick?"

"Yes," she nodded. "Actually it was three minutes to six, though I don't suppose that matters."

"Everything matters. The train left Liverpool Street at 5.57. And arrived at Benwick?"

"At a quarter past eight."

"Did you walk back to the house?"

"I think I ran part of the way."

"You were in a hurry to get back?"

"Yes, though somehow I dreaded it, too. I don't know why. I'm afraid I always seem to be saying that. It was a relief not to be going to Boulogne, but I was in such a state that even the house didn't seem to be much better. When I got there—"

"Did you meet any one?"

"No. It's rather a lonely road. When I got there I took out my key, and then I did the silliest thing of all—which shows the foolish state I was in. I fumbled with it and dropped it, and it went down a little grating. Of course, that finished it. It was no good ringing, because there was no one inside to let me in."

Hazeldean wondered!

"So then what?" he inquired.

"I didn't give up at once. When I found I couldn't get the key back—well, I did try ringing, just on the chance. But my uncle wasn't there. Then I thought of the french window. There's one round the side, from the drawing-room." She paused for an instant. "It wasn't any use. Uncle had put the shutters across."

"I suppose you always leave the windows shuttered when you go away?" he asked, making his voice as casual as he could.

"No, never," she answered. "I don't know why he did it this time."

"So, of course, you couldn't get in that way. Did you try anywhere else?"

"No. All at once I felt—quite definitely—that I didn't want to." She gave a little shudder. "When a cat ran by, I nearly jumped out of my skin."

"That doesn't surprise me. A completely dark house—even when it's your own—wouldn't be very pleasant under those circumstances. If there'd been a light anywhere you'd have known that somebody—your uncle—was inside."

Again he spoke as casually as he could. He was wondering whether the lights in the drawing-room had been on at that time, and whether she had glimpsed them through the shutters.

"Yes, of course," she said.

"What did you do next?"

"I went back to the station and just caught the last train back to London. It got in at a quarter past eleven. I booked a room at the station hotel, and next day—this morning—I came to Boulogne. I got here in time for lunch—and a lecture from my uncle. He said he'd been worried stiff."

"He must have been anxious," answered Hazeldean. "I suppose you told him all that had happened—just as you've told me?"

"Yes," she replied.

"What I can't make out," he went on, "is why your uncle didn't turn back when he found you weren't on the train."

"Yes, Madame Paula gave it to him hot for that," smiled Dora. "But it really wasn't his fault; it was quite simple. He thought I must have taken an earlier train to Folkestone, and that I'd be waiting for him there; and anyhow the train doesn't stop on the way. Then, when he didn't find me at Folkestone station, he thought I must be on the boat."

"But when he found you weren't?"

"The boat had started—like the train. You see, he wasted most of the time looking for me at the station… And that's all," she concluded. "And now it's your turn."

"No, not just for a moment," answered Hazeldean. "Have you had any trouble since you arrived here?"

"What do you mean?"

"Well—Dr. Jones—"

"I've not seen him yet. He was away when I arrived."

"Yes, I remember, you told me. And your uncle went out after lunch. Hallo, perhaps this is him back again."

Someone had knocked at the front door. The sound echoed eerily to them through dim passages. In response to his raised eyebrows, Dora Fenner shook her head.

"He wouldn't knock," she murmured nervously.

"Nor would Dr. Jones," he replied, "so it must be somebody else. Probably someone inquiring for rooms, eh?"

A sound came from the passage. It was a soft sound, and it began too near the parlour door for Hazeldean's comfort. A vaguely rustling sound, that conjured the vision of Madame Paula—he visualised her, large-bosomed, voluptuous and over-complexioned—moving away to answer the knock.

He turned to the window and glanced out cautiously. He got a glimpse of the visitor. It was the dark-skinned vendor of silks.

CHAPTER IX

Madame Paula

TURNING HIS HEAD AND GLANCING BACK INTO THE ROOM, he saw Dora's eyes, big, round, startled. He knew by her expression that he had not sufficiently guarded his own.

"Who is it?" she whispered.

"Just one of those street merchants," he replied. "I suppose you often get them here?"

"I've never known one call before," she answered.

They waited, and heard, faintly, a door open. Then voices conversing, but sliced by the acoustics. One—low, suave—came to them sideways along an outside wall; the other—quick and sharp—reached them via interior passages. The words of neither were audible in the parlour. They formed an incoherent, ill-matched duet.

The duet ended abruptly. The door slammed, making the parlour door tremble for a moment through the impact. Silence followed.

"Madame Paula hasn't moved," reflected Hazeldean. "She's still standing just inside the front door. I'd give a fortune to know what she's feeling!"

Suddenly he gave the window curtain a little jerk, to pull it farther across the glass, and retreated into the middle of the parlour. A figure went by the window slowly, making a vague smudge. The footsteps died away.

"Aren't you *ever* going to tell me!"

Something inside the girl was snapping.

"Yes—I must now," he answered.

A draught, or feeling of space, made him swing round towards the door. It was open, and a woman stood in the passage, looking in upon them. He knew it was Madame Paula at once. She was so exactly as he had pictured her. Her large bosom almost filled the width of the doorway, and her high complexion and too-gold hair loomed unnaturally, almost garishly, in the dimness. The air became heavily scented. Perhaps the scent, also, had made him turn. The one thing that had not made him turn was sound. Madame Paula had reached the door and opened it noiselessly.

"I was wrong," thought Hazeldean. "She wasn't standing just inside the front door. She was on her way here!"

"Oh, a visitor!" said the unpleasant woman, with feigned surprise.

Dora broke in quickly.

"Yes, he came to inquire the way," she exclaimed, "and I'm letting him see a map."

Her voice sounded breathless. Hazeldean got an uneasy impression that she was losing her head, and that she not merely disliked Madame Paula, but dreaded her.

"She's been very kind," he added to the girl's statement. "I was utterly lost."

"Well, have you found your way now?" asked Madame Paula.

She spoke English well, with only a slight accent.

"Sufficiently, for the moment," he answered. "But Boulogne takes some knowing. It's a delightful place."

"So people say who don't live in it."

"Not having lived in it myself, I stick to my opinion. By the way, am I right? Is this a pension?"

"Mais oui!"

"Avez vous un chambre, si je le desire? Now, you see that my French isn't as good as your English. I like this spot so much, I thought I might perhaps spend a night here."

Madame Paula did not respond at once. She gave a quick glance at Dora, who was unable to conceal her sudden pleasure in the suggestion. He would not have made it if he had not divined her approval in advance.

"A room," repeated Madame Paula. "Why—yes—it might be managed."

He had expected a refusal.

"You're not quite full up, then?"

"I think I have one room vacant, m'sieur. Perhaps I could show it to you?"

"Now?"

"Why not?"

He could think of no reason why not, yet he discovered a queer reluctance within himself to leave the room, and he attributed it to over-anxiety regarding the girl's safety during his absence.

"You'll come back?" said Dora. "I want to talk to you about the Notre Dame—you must see that!"

"Thank you, I'll be back," he answered. "All this is most fortune—I'm in luck."

He followed Madame Paula out into the passage. He wished she had not been so particular to close the door. They walked for a moment or two in silence. In the narrow passage he found the woman's scent almost nauseating. "But if I were another sort of a man," he told himself, "I would find it delicious. Does Mr. Fenner find it delicious?" Suddenly Madame Paula spoke.

"I am not sure about the luck," she said, with a kind of hard directness. "Did you notice she is a little—as you say—not all there?"

"I certainly did not notice it," responded Hazeldean.

"Well, it is true."

She touched her forehead, then gave a little shrug. On the point of expressing incredulity, Hazeldean changed his tactics. It occurred to him that by diplomacy he might add to his knowledge.

"How tragic!" he said. "And how nice of you to look after her. If she is weak-minded, I am sure she cannot be a relative!"

If he hoped Madame Paula would melt under the fatuous compliment, he was disappointed. She continued in her hard voice—he was sure she had another voice more in keeping with her scent:

"Has she been telling you things?"

"Yes."

"Ah!"

"The way about Boulogne."

"I do not mean that!" she frowned.

"What other things should she tell me—a stranger?" he replied.

"But that is what I say—she is not normal," retorted Madame Paula almost impatiently. They had reached the front hall now, and she had stopped. "If she told you any other things, you would not believe them?"

"Madame Paula—" he began.

"Oh, you know my name," she interrupted.

"It is over your door. How can I say whether I would believe things or not till I know what the things are? All this is very mysterious! May I know what's in your mind, so I can be warned when I go back to her?"

Madame Paula's frown grew.

"But—you will see—it would not be wise to go back to her," she exclaimed.

"Oh, come—"

"Listen! I know! It is best to go."

"But you are showing me a room—"

"I have no room. That was an excuse. She is tired, excited. Believe me, m'sieur, I know her well, and I know when she needs to be quiet. I will tell her you did not like the room, and that you found it was late—and you asked me to make your excuses."

She moved towards the front door as she spoke. He did not follow her. When she got to the door she turned, with her hand on the knob.

"Well?" she rasped.

He shook his head good-humouredly.

"I believe you've got a room," he insisted.

"And why should I say I have not, if I have?"

"Because you're afraid I will excite Miss Fenner—"

"Oh! You know her name, too?"

"We introduced ourselves. But don't worry. If I take the room there will be no need for me to disturb her—"

Madame Paula stamped her foot.

"*Mon Dieu!*" she cried. "Are you, too, weak in the head?"

Dora Fenner was not the only person in Madame Paula's pension, Hazeldean decided, who was suffering from nerves this afternoon.

"If I am weak in the head, it is all the more necessary for me to cover the sensitive headpiece," he remarked smoothly. "I have left my hat in Miss Fenner's room."

She looked at him suspiciously, as though aware that he had not worn a hat.

"Well, wait and I will get it."

She turned and sped past him quickly, and came back with suspicious speed.

"It is not there," she said.

"I'll look myself," he retorted.

She barred the way. He saw she was growing flustered, and as she lost her assurance he began to show his.

"Madame Paula," he said, changing his tone, "that hat was an excuse, like your room. You didn't have a room, and I didn't have a hat. But if I cannot see Miss Fenner, I shall wait to see her uncle, Mr. Fenner, and you will be wise to raise no more objections. I've brought some very terrible news."

Madame Paula's too-red mouth opened. He watched her crumple with uncharitable satisfaction.

"What—news?" she stammered.

"You will forgive me," he answered firmly.

She breathed hard for several seconds. Then, regaining a little of her lost composure, she said:

"Very well, m'sieur. I am a helpless woman, and I can do nothing. Yes, I have a room. It is right, I see now, that you should have it. Please come this way."

She turned and invited him towards another passage. He followed her along it, and they mounted a twisting flight of stairs. At the top she paused.

"Have you told Miss Fenner yet?" she asked.

"Not yet," he replied.

"I think that is well, m'sieur. Perhaps she could not stand it. Her uncle should be told first—he will know how to pass it to her. Terrible news? *Mon Dieu!* You will pardon my rudeness, m'sieur. But how was I to know, when you took so long to—?"

Her voice trailed off. She moved on to a small door.

"This is the best I have," she muttered, pushing the door open. "I will tell Mr. Fenner as soon as he returns. Any minute now. Such things make one weak. My legs are jelly!"

She stood aside as he went into the room. It was an attic, with a small window in a sloping roof.

"Is this really all you have?" he asked.

He received no answer. She had vanished, and he heard the key turning softly in the lock.

CHAPTER X

Mr. Fenner

DURING THE MOMENTS IMMEDIATELY FOLLOWING MADAME Paula's startlingly swift departure, Tom Hazeldean passed through many equally swift emotions.

The first was self-anger. He was angrier with himself than he was with Madame Paula, for his ego was humiliated by a sense of inefficiency. "Am I as smart as I thought I was?" he asked himself. "Am I a bungler outside my boat? What would Kendall think of me, allowing myself to be locked in a room by a confounded woman?" He had scored one victory over the confounded woman, but she had duped him and prepared the way for a greater victory even while he had been congratulating himself.

Then a new emotion came to his aid. If he had been a fool, she had really been little cleverer, for she had declared her hand by definitely starting a war. There was something exhilarating in that fact. Action was far more to his liking than manœuvring, and the obvious action before him was to escape from the attic and confront Madame Paula again—this time without finesse. For all her momentary triumph, she must be in a fine panic! She could hardly expect him to wait quietly for his release. Probably she was listening now for his ominous banging on the door or his shouts...

Then came a third emotion—fear. Not for himself, but for Dora Fenner. Madame Paula's desperation might not end at locking a door. Perhaps at this moment she was hurrying to Dora's parlour, urged by unintelligent terror to some new act. It was the third emotion that ended his inactivity and took him back to the door.

He did not bang on it. If Madame Paula had shown her hand, there was no need for him to show his until the situation forced it. It would be useful if she believed he had not yet discovered he was a prisoner—she had turned the key softly in the hope of delaying that discovery—and it might postpone her next move. So, with equal softness, he turned the handle and tested the lock's firmness.

The lock was a depressingly stout one, and the door looked as stout as the lock.

Well, what about the window? He glanced at the sloping roof. He could not quite reach the glass from the floor, but a chair gave him the necessary height, and in a few seconds he had eased the tightness round the little frame and pushed it upwards. He stared up into blue sky. A startled pigeon swooped away as his head came through the aperture in the roof. Now he stared at other roofs, though none near enough for a jump. Turning his head to the right, he saw narrow, sleepy roads below. They were too far below to reach without risking a broken leg. On the left the ground was higher, for the shorter wall on this side began on the ramparts. While he was reckoning his chances, he saw something that made him pause. The dark-skinned silk vendor standing in a shadow. Still hanging around.

"I wish I could place that fellow!" thought Hazeldean, moving his head to the concealment of a chimney-pot. "He's stalking me, obviously, and he knows I'm somewhere about. If I shout, that will bring him along as well as others. Hell—this isn't so easy! Thomas Hazeldean, you're in a jam. I'm beginning to wonder, very seriously, whether the world gained in brain-power when you were born!"

A grey-haired man came round an angle of the ramparts. He wore a large black squash felt, but the grey hair was almost professorially long, and its untidy edges escaped beneath the hat's rim. The man's face was also grey, and he walked with a slight stoop.

The silk vendor did not move from his shadow. The grey-haired man did not appear to notice him, although there was something odd in his manner—something almost furtively casual. Unless Hazeldean, in a mood to notice everything, was noticing more than actually existed? The grey-haired man stopped at the door of the pension. He gave a quick glance backwards and forwards along the rampart path. If he now noticed the figure in the shadow, he still gave no sign of it, but felt in his pocket for a key. He brought the key out just before advancing to the door and becoming invisible from the point where Hazeldean was watching. An edge of the roof shut him abruptly from view.

"Key," thought Hazeldean. "Dr. Jones?"

He heard the door open below. It sounded surprisingly close. As it closed—he did not hear any voices—the silk vendor began to move forward out of the shadow. Impulsively, Hazeldean ducked down on his chair. After a moment's reflection, he quietly closed the skylight, descended to the floor, replaced the chair in its original position and waited.

"Five minutes," he decided. "No longer."

He was obeying instinct now. The new-comer would start a fresh train of events inside the house, and might divert Madame Paula from any immediate rashness. He wanted to give the new events their chance, but his ears were not going to miss anything they could catch, and he stole to the attic door and listened.

The five minutes ticked slowly away. He timed them by his watch. It was something to do during the painful inactivity of waiting. He had to keep his imagination in check, for it had begun to paint exaggerated pictures. He hoped, at least, they were exaggerated; the canvas of reality was grim enough. Neatly, as the fifth minute was ending, steps sounded in the passage. He drew back from the door, keeping his eyes upon it. The footsteps stopped outside the door, a key was turned and the door opened. The grey-haired man stood in the doorway looking at him.

The scrutiny did not last long. The grey-haired man spoke almost at once.

"I have to apologise," he said. "I am afraid we are all a little upset to-day. But it was—of course—a mistake to lock you in. Unwarrantable!"

"Well, I can't disagree with that," answered Hazeldean. "Are you Dr. Jones?"

"Dr. Jones?" repeated the grey-haired man slowly. "No, I am not Dr. Jones. Nor, at this moment, do I particularly want to be. I am Mr. Fenner. I think you have some news for me?"

So this was the owner of Haven House, at last! The uncle of Dora Fenner…

"May I hear what this news is?"

"Yes, of course," said Hazeldean. "You have no idea what I have come about?"

"How should I? Not the slightest."

"It is grave news."

"Indeed? Then it fits the day. I have just brought some grave news myself. You must not expect to see Madame Paula again. She has retired to her room. Her husband—Dr. Jones—is dead."

While he absorbed this information, Hazeldean murmured,

"How shocking. I'm terribly sorry." But there was no sympathy in his heart. He had only recently heard of Dr. Jones, and what he had heard was not to his liking. Instead of sympathy, he felt a kind of startled curiosity. Was this fresh tragedy a coincidence, merely an example of the axiom: "It never rains but it pours?" Or could it have any connection with other happenings?

"It was an accident," continued Mr. Fenner. He did not seem to be suffering from much sympathy himself, though this might be self-control, or a concession to a disinterested stranger. "His aeroplane crashed a few miles from here. But there's no need to worry you with that. Yes? This other news? Has my house burned down?"

"No, but something else has happened there."

"Well?"

"Some people have been found dead in your house—"

"I beg your pardon?"

"Seven of them."

Mr. Fenner's eyebrows went up. Then he smiled.

"And now, please, explain the joke," he suggested.

"I'm afraid it isn't a joke," answered Hazeldean.

"I see. Someone I have never seen tells me that seven people I do not know—at least, I presume I do not know them—have died in my house, and I am expected to believe it. Seven is a somewhat large number, sir! And they must have taken possession of my house and died in it exceedingly quickly! I was in the house myself yesterday at a quarter to one, and it was certainly empty when I left it. Perhaps—after this—I may let you into the secret of why you were locked in this room. You alarmed Madame Paula, and she came to the conclusion—forgive me for mentioning it—that you were mad."

"I will certainly forgive you for mentioning it," replied Hazeldean, "because, if you shared Madame Paula's opinion, you obviously wouldn't do so."

"I wonder if that is as clever as it sounds?" mused Mr. Fenner. His tone had become a little impersonal. "Would I not?"

"Not unless—forgive *me* for suggesting it—you were also mad yourself."

Mr. Fenner frowned.

"I am not sure that I appreciate this conversation," he said.

"I am quite sure I don't," retorted Hazeldean. "So what about ending it? I expect, after all, I should have left it to the police, who are in your house at this moment, and from whom, of course, you will hear. Meanwhile, if you're not interested, that's your affair, not mine. By the way, the police are particularly curious about an old cricket ball—and the drawing-room shutters. Good-afternoon."

He hoped, as he moved, that the bluff would succeed. It succeeded instantaneously. Mr. Fenner closed the door and stood before it.

"What the devil's all this?" he exclaimed.

"I'm trying to tell you," responded Hazeldean. "Do you know anything about a cricket ball?"

"God above! I am told of seven dead people in my house, and then I'm expected to be interested in a cricket ball! Perhaps I do know something about a cricket ball! Perhaps I don't! Why should I tell you? But—shutters? Drawing-room shutters?" He moved closer to Hazeldean and stared at him hard. "I retract any suggestion of your madness, sir. You look sane enough. Now tell your story. No, wait. What's your name?"

"Thomas Hazeldean."

"Thank you—Hazeldean. Are you connected with the police?"

"No—I come into this by mere chance."

"I see. Let us hope it will prove a fortunate chance! Pray proceed. If there are truly seven dead people in my private residence, it is right—I admit—that I should hear about it!"

He motioned Hazeldean to a chair and then sat down himself, breathing rather heavily.

Hazeldean told his story.

CHAPTER XI

Sequel to a Cricket Ball

MR. FENNER DID NOT SPEAK FOR A FULL MINUTE AFTER Hazeldean had completed his narration. His grey eyebrows were lowered over his grey eyes, and his pupils, piercing the floor towards which they were directed, were almost hidden by stiff, wiry hairs. Hazeldean had no clue to what he was thinking. The listener had spoken no word, and revealed nothing by his expression.

Suddenly the pupils contracted, their focus shortened, and Mr. Fenner exclaimed, "The thing's incredible!"

"But true," added Hazeldean.

"I must believe it. But—seven people committing suicide—"

"That's not so necessary to believe."

"What do you mean?" exclaimed Mr. Fenner sharply.

"Just that the police aren't banking on that theory," answered Hazeldean. "But, of course, they're not excluding it."

"They'd be fools if they did—with that written confession!"

"There was something on the other side of the paper."

"Yes. Please repeat that—if you're sure you've remembered it correctly."

"'With apologies from the Suicide Club' on one side," repeated Hazeldean, "and—in what looked like a different scrawl—'Particulars at address 59·16S 4·6E G,' on the other."

"Odd sort of address!"

"Very."

"What did the police make of it?"

"They didn't say."

"What do you make of it?"

"Nothing. What do you?"

"No more than you do! Probably some message in cipher."

"But if the writer was trying to write a message," asked Hazeldean, "why should he conceal his meaning?"

Mr. Fenner threw up his hands.

"Why should seven people walk into my house and kill themselves?" he retorted. "Why anything? Unless we are dealing with madness—which itself upsets all logic." He paused, then added slowly, "Why the cricket ball?"

"Yes, but you've got some theory about that," answered Hazeldean, taking a chance shot.

"What makes you think so?" demanded Mr. Fenner.

"Just a guess," admitted Hazeldean, "but I'm willing to wager it's a good guess."

"Before I tell you whether it is a good guess or a bad guess," said Mr. Fenner, "may I know a little more about that fellow you mentioned at the end of your story? The fellow you thought was shadowing you."

"Oh, the silk merchant," replied Hazeldean. He had referred to him briefly.

"Yes. I think I saw the man as I came in just now."

"You did."

"Eh? You know that?"

Hazeldean smiled.

"When you are locked in a room, you test all the possible exits."

He glanced at the skylight. Mr. Fenner's eyes followed him.

"I see," he murmured. "Or, rather, *you* saw. So he's shadowed you all the way from the quay?"

"It seems like it."

"And you've no notion why?"

"Not the remotest."

Mr. Fenner nodded, got up from his chair and walked slowly to the door and back. He was thinking hard.

"I must go back at once," he said; "but before I go I will tell you something that I shall also tell the police. The reason I did not mention it before, Mr. Hazeldean, was because—well, it was natural—you will agree, I think—because I wanted to hear all you had to say first. You were a stranger to me. I had no reason to confide in you. On the contrary I had some reason to doubt you—as you will understand in a moment. And, moreover, what I am about to tell you has so far been told to no one—not even my niece. It concerns—the cricket ball. You say, by the way, that it was on top of a silver vase?"

"Yes," replied Hazeldean.

"I did not put it there. Some queer irony is behind all this. Among all the unanswered whys and wherefores we must include the position of this cricket ball. It symbolises something—but what?" He frowned, then shrugged his shoulders. "A little while ago I received an anonymous letter. It was in printed writing—similar, I take it, to the admission of suicide. It said, 'One day you will receive a cricket ball. When that happens, be advised, and clear out.' Just that. What would you have done?"

"We never know what we would do till the occasion arises," answered Hazeldean non-committally. "I might have taken it to the police."

"So might I," responded Mr. Fenner dryly. "But I did not. The thing was too ridiculous. I threw it on the fire."

"That was a pity."

"I agree. At the time, however, I had no desire to risk ridicule.

I am already regarded locally as something of an eccentric. That is always, perhaps, the fate of a man who does not fraternise—who prefers thought to company. When a second communication came, I did the same thing. I burned it. I was annoyed and angry, and still assumed the whole thing was a silly practical joke. Yesterday morning, being tired and overworked, I suggested coming here. My niece was not—enthusiastic. But when the cricket ball arrived—it was my niece who found it—something snapped inside me, and—I admit—I was disturbed. My niece's mood changed. I expect she realised that I needed the change. She said she was willing to come to Boulogne. So I accepted the situation—and that is all I can tell you… I see a question coming. Let me forestall it. The police—why did I still not go to them?"

"Yes, I think I should have gone that time," said Hazeldean.

"And I intended to go that time," answered Mr. Fenner. "I packed my niece off quickly, told her I would follow, and was glad to see her out of the house. I did not give her my real reason for telling her to go at once. I suggested she should do some shopping in London, and meant to visit the police station before joining her on the boat train. But when the time came for me to leave the house myself—well, somehow or other—tell me, Mr. Hazeldean, have you *seen* our local sergeant?"

"I have."

"Does he strike you as a man burdened down by brains?"

"I wouldn't quite put it like that."

"I am sure you would not! And, having seen him, can you visualise his attitude—his face—when I informed him that I was leaving my house because a cricket ball had suddenly appeared there, and would he kindly keep an eye on the place till I returned? The two communications giving significance to the ball were burnt. Do you think—frankly—he would have been very helpful?"

"You wouldn't have had to depend on him," replied Hazeldean. "The case is in the hands of a far smarter man—Inspector Kendall, if you know him."

"I do not know him."

"Well, he's in charge."

"I am glad to hear it, if he is as smart as you suggest. But I had no knowledge of this at the time. I came away—leaving my premises empty, it appears, for the next meeting of a suicide club! But one member does not seem to have committed suicide."

"Who?"

"Our silk merchant."

"Now *you're* guessing!" said Hazeldean.

"Of course I am," retorted Mr. Fenner; "but maybe I can guess as well as you can! That fellow worries me. I am not going to take my niece back to Haven House till this matter has been cleared up; but I don't like the idea of leaving her here alone if that fellow's going to remain hanging around!... Would *you*, in my place?"

He fixed Hazeldean quizzically with his eyes.

"Not particularly," admitted Hazeldean.

"I suggest that is putting it mildly?"

"Very mildly."

Mr. Fenner rubbed his nose thoughtfully, then went on:

"You have been very good, Mr. Hazeldean. I will not pretend to understand why—whether it is your natural disposition to help people, or whether you have some—some special interest you have not explained." He paused, and the quizzical eyes grew more quizzical, then suddenly seemed to dismiss the inquiry within them. "The fact remains. You have sailed from Essex to Boulogne in your boat—did you mention its name—?"

"The *Spray*."

"*Spray*. Rather an apt name. Spray splashes where the wave takes it, and you—so to speak—have splashed here. Though, I confess, you do not look to me like a young man who merely obeys the tide. Otherwise I should not make the request I am about to make. Do you feel inclined to help us further?"

"Certainly, if I can," answered Hazeldean.

"You can."

"How?"

"I am very worried about Dora—my niece. I think you already understand my predicament." Hazeldean nodded. "Would it be asking too much of you to remain with her here in this pension till I return—or, at any rate, till I have had time to learn the position at home first hand, and can make the wisest arrangements for her? You have already put yourself out for us more than it would have been reasonable to expect. You have prepared me for a most formidable ordeal. I have no right to ask you to put yourself out any more. But, if you stayed, it would greatly ease my mind—and you could, of course, take a room here. For that matter, you could have mine… Well?"

Hazeldean was hesitating. His hesitation was not due to any unwillingness to stay; it was just because the idea appealed to him so strongly that he did not want to risk being blinded by his personal desires. He was already fighting certain uneasy self-doubts. The vision of Inspector Kendall's solemn, responsible face was a little too insistent. He did not want to make it more solemn. Having developed the situation to its present point, he had to justify what he had done by avoiding errors.

Still, he could not see anything against Mr. Fenner's suggestion. On the contrary, the more he considered it, the more reasonable it appeared. The idea of leaving Dora Fenner here was as distasteful to him as to her uncle.

"I see I have asked too much," said Mr. Fenner with a little sigh. "Forgive me."

"No, you haven't asked too much," replied Hazeldean quickly. "I'm just wondering—"

"Yes?"

"Whether it's the wisest plan."

"Have you a wiser?"

"I could take you all back in my boat."

"I confess I had thought of that. But the problem of Dora remains when we get over. I positively refuse to take her into the middle of all this—ghastliness; or anywhere near it, for that matter. You know what it would be like. Even if she were not pestered by the police. The publicity! She's in no condition for that sort of thing. I doubt whether she could stand it."

"Could I take her to friends?"

But Mr. Fenner again shook his head.

"This may surprise you, Mr. Hazeldean. We have no friends. None, at any rate, whom I could leave her with. You can believe me when I assure you that—provided she is safe, and has someone with her—she will be much better staying quietly here—at present. Still, I do not press my request, naturally. I should not have made it—that is, I might not have made it—if Madame Paula had been in a better condition to look after her. Unfortunately, now Madame Paula has a tragedy of her own."

"Yes, what about Madame Paula?" asked Hazeldean. "Wouldn't *she* prefer it if we all left? Instead—just now—of having a new guest saddled on her?"

"That is a point," admitted Mr. Fenner, "although, of course, there is a staff here. There would be no need for her to be worried. Still—wait a moment."

He left the room abruptly. In three minutes he was back.

"I have just seen Madame Paula," he said. "We are old friends—yes, I made a mistake when I said we had no friends—I meant, of course, in England—and Madame Paula is quite agreeable. In fact, she agrees with me that it would be unwise for Dora to leave here just yet. She would like you to stay—if you can forgive her," he added, with a faint smile, "for her original reception of you."

"Naturally—of course," replied Hazeldean. "And, in that case—"

"You consent?"

Hazeldean nodded.

"Mr. Hazeldean, you have taken a great load off my mind!" Mr. Fenner exclaimed. "I am more relieved than I can say! And now, since that is fixed, I must get busy. I have to take Madame Paula to the police station—she has to identify her husband—what remains of him—and she wishes to get that over as soon as possible. Naturally, I said I would go with her. From the police station I shall telephone through to Benwick, get the latest information, and tell them I am coming—"

"How will you go?"

"By the boat."

"What about an aeroplane?"

"Thank you, no! I have a horror of the air—and I am about to accompany a lady to see the remains of her husband who has crashed! I have never been up in the air, and I never intend to go. These days, the ground is quite unsafe enough for me!"

"Well, there's a boat at 7.20."

"Yes, I know. It gets into Victoria at eleven. The train, that is, not the boat. You will forgive me if I am a little distrait. Seven-twenty will just give me time to put a few things into my bag, to see to Madame Paula's business and to get to the quay. If I go at once.

But first I must have a talk with my niece, and let her know what has been arranged." Suddenly he shot a question which seemed to come rather late in the day. "Does my niece know about all this?"

"I was on the point of telling her when Madame Paula interrupted us," answered Hazeldean.

"Then I will tell her." He looked at his watch. "I must hurry. Do you know where the dining-room is? I'll send the maid to you. She will get you some tea, and afterwards my room will be free—No. 4—and perhaps you would see my niece."

"I'll need a few things from my boat," Hazeldean reminded him.

"Of course—that's a nuisance," replied Mr. Fenner, frowning. "Is there any one in the boat?"

"A man and a boy."

"Could one of them bring your things along, if I delivered a message for you?"

"You won't have time. You're going to be busy!"

"I could do it. And if you go to the boat yourself—well, it will take you some little while from here, and I'm afraid I should be gone before you came back. I dare say I am over-anxious. Of course, there's the staff—but a half-witted maid and an old man falling to bits are not much protection for my niece if our silk merchant makes trouble after we all depart!"

"But you don't really think the fellow is menacing your niece, do you?" inquired Hazeldean.

"My dear fellow, I do not know what I think!" exclaimed Mr. Fenner, throwing up his hands. "I did not think seven people would be found dead in my house! I did not think Madame Paula's husband would choose the occasion to crash in his aeroplane! I did not think I should be talking to a stranger in an attic, and putting my only relative in his charge! All I do know, sir—though I am doing my best to control myself, and my best is not now quite as good as it was—is that I am distracted!"

He looked it. His original calmness had gone, as though dissipated by the grim facts that were crowding around him. For the first time he induced Hazeldean's sympathy.

"I am not as young as you, Mr. Hazeldean," he added in a quieter tone, "and I have been working hard lately—overworking. Perhaps my condition is not very much better than my niece's. We came here for a rest. That is rather comic, isn't it?"

He gave a mirthless laugh.

"I'll stay here," said Hazeldean. "I'll write a letter to my man—Blythe's the name—"

"And the boat is the *Spray*, you mentioned?"

"Yes. Blythe can come along with my bag. As a matter of fact, I'd like to see him. Probably I'll find him plenty to do."

He explained the position of the boat. Mr. Fenner said he knew the spot, and produced a sheet of notepaper for the note. A minute later the agitated man Fenner had departed, and Hazeldean was being conducted by a bovine, vaguely attractive maid, alleged to possess only half her wits, along a narrow, twisting passage to a low-ceilinged dining-room.

CHAPTER XII

Interlude in a Dining-Room

THE DINING-ROOM HAD NOT BEEN DESIGNED FOR BRIGHTNESS. Hazeldean chose a table by the one window, but the view was disappointing. He looked out through heavy lace curtains on a small deep yard, closed in by walls that gave it the appearance of a pit. "I wonder if anything really happy has ever happened in this spot?" came the thought. If gloom could be stored and passed on through the generations, the spot on which Madame Paula's pension had grown had certainly preserved it. Perhaps, at some period in the history of Boulogne—when the high walls had been stormed with battering rams and scaling ladders, and the attackers had been repelled with burning oil—some particularly terrible incident had happened here to leave an indelible mark. He contrasted the room with his cosy cabin, the delight of which had withstood the menace of wind and storm and mountainous seas. Places were sometimes like people, shaping incidents to their moods.

Yet, in spite of its brooding atmosphere, the dining-room had a queer attraction. So had the bovine maid, with her heavy, dormant beauty. After accompanying him to his table, she had departed for the tea, and now she was returning with a tray. Well, the contents of the tray looked good enough, and would help to while away a rather anxious quarter of an hour.

Part of the anxiety was due to the persistence of his self-doubts. "Should I be sitting here?" he wondered uneasily. "Isn't there something else I could be doing?" Yet, for the life of him, he could not think what it was. His problem was becoming more and more centralised in the safety of Dora Fenner, imprisoned—that seemed the right word—amid these grim surroundings and unsatisfactory people. If any other duty called him, it would probably lie outside the pension, and for the time being he was refusing to go outside—unless Dora Fenner came with him…

The maid put the tray down on the table.

"Do you speak English?" asked Hazeldean.

"Leetle, mais not mooch," she answered.

"Et mois, je parle not mooch French," he smiled. "Vous avez charmonte place ici."

She smiled back, seeming rather surprised, either at the compliment to the place or to herself. Possibly she was not accustomed to polite conversation with strangers, although in a pension she should have been.

"Avez vous telephone ici?" asked Hazeldean.

"Non, m'sieur," she said. "Eet is—" She could not find the word. "Long way."

The news did not surprise him, for it confirmed the impression he had received from Mr. Fenner. If there had been a telephone, he need not have waited to get through to Benwick from the police station. And there would have presumably been some advance telephonic communication about the tragedy of Dr. Jones… Yes… Dr. Jones… How were others reacting to the tragedy of Dr. Jones?

"Monsieur Fenner, il me dit de Dr. Jones," he said. "C'est tragique."

"Oui, c'est terrible," answered the maid.

Her rather thick eyebrows descended in a frown, but she did not display any personal grief. It was bad news, as one might read in a newspaper.

"J'espère que Madame n'est pas—trop—qu'est-ce que c'est upset? Malade?"

"Malade! Domage, elle est très malade! Zey tell me, but I'ave not see 'er."

"Dans sa chambre, n'est-ce pas?"

His questions were aimless, but he wanted to keep her talking. The desire was frustrated by the sudden appearance in the dark doorway of a very old man.

"Marie, venez ici!" he cried. "Vite!"

"Pardon," murmured the maid, and vanished.

Hazeldean kept his eyes on the door, now closed, while their footsteps faded away; Marie's quick and heavy, the old man's shuffling. "Assuming that was Pierre," reflected Hazeldean, "now I've seen the lot. Pierre and Marie. I don't mind Marie, though I could quite easily live without her, but I don't like Pierre. Why don't I like Pierre? Just the nasty, suspicious nature I'm developing? Why on earth does Mr. Fenner bring his niece to this very unpleasant place?"

Feeling more and more disturbed, he began his meal. The tea was as good as he would have expected in England, and he could not complain of the rolls and the toast and the *gateaux*, but they gave him no enjoyment. Somewhere in a cobbled street outside, distant but distinct, a piano-organ tinkled. The intermezzo from *Cavalleria Rusticana*. It gave him a sense that nothing moved here save primitive, unseen things.

"And I'm not moving, either!" he exclaimed aloud.

Abruptly he jumped up, following an instinct that reversed his previous policy, but as he neared the dining-room door he heard the sound of shuffling. Recognising it, he returned quickly to the table and rang a little hand-bell. He was seated again when Pierre materialised once more in the doorway.

The old man stopped, blinking at Hazeldean like an ancient, furrowed owl.

"Do you speak English?" Hazeldean called.

"Non, m'sieur," answered Pierre.

"Then how the devil do you know what I've just asked?" demanded Hazeldean.

The ancient owl became a trifle more furrowed, and then repeated: "Non, m'sieur."

"Meaning, exactly?"

"Non, m'sieur."

Hazeldean mistrusted his attitude. There was no perplexity in the old man's vaguely apologetic smile.

"Then if I were to offer you a hundred pounds to direct me at once to the nearest telephone, you would not be able to earn it?"

"Pardon?"

"All right, have it your own way. Ou est Monsieur Fenner?"

"Il est parti, m'sieur."

"Already?"

"Pardon?"

"Et Madame?"

"Aussi."

If this were true, the reversed policy would have to be reconsidered, for it meant that Dora Fenner was already alone with her unsatisfactory bodyguard.

"Ou est Mademoiselle Fenner?"

"Ma'm'selle Fenner? Mais—dans sa chambre, m'sieur."

Pierre's raised eyebrows added mutely, "Where else should she be?"

"I see." Hazeldean paused, then went on, in an audible mutter, as though to himself: "Nuisance, the others have gone. How am

I going to get this news to 'em about Dr. Jones? It's vital to them, too!"

Watching closely, Hazeldean noted Pierre's expression change at the name "Dr. Jones."

"Ah, le pauvre homme!" murmured Pierre. "Tragique—tragique!"

Hazeldean thought, "This damn rascal's beating me! He's cleverer than his fellow-domestic—he had the sense to realise that, even if he couldn't speak English, he'd recognise the name of his late master when I mentioned it!"

But perhaps, after all, he *couldn't* speak English?

Giving it up, Hazeldean rose. Pierre, still standing in the doorway, glanced at the table.

"Finis, m'sieur?"

"Yes, thanks. Oui, merci."

"Mais non!" The tone was deprecating. Too many cakes remained on the dish. "Vous n'etes pas content?"

"Oui, everything was delightful," answered Hazeldean. "Charmonte."

"Merci. Numero Quatre, m'sieur. S'il vous plait?"

He turned as Hazeldean reached him, and hobbled ahead. Hazeldean followed till he found himself in a spot he recognised, and knew that the direction he wanted was not Pierre's.

"Pas numero Quatre," he said.

"Mais oui, Quatre," insisted Pierre.

"Non. Pas encore. Je vais voir Mademoiselle Fenner."

The old man stopped abruptly, peered at Hazeldean as though to make sure that he meant what he said, and then smiled.

"Un moment, m'sieur. Je vais voir—"

In that moment he had vanished.

"Confound the fellow!" muttered Hazeldean.

He darted after him. He was not going to let Pierre win all along the line. Round a bend he nearly ran into the maid.

"Oh, m'sieur!" gasped the maid.

"What's the matter?" demanded Hazeldean.

Marie put her hand to her heart. She was breathless. A belief that she was purposely obstructing his progress lasted only an instant. Her distracted condition was genuine.

"She is faint," panted Marie.

"Who? Miss Fenner?"

Marie nodded as Hazeldean dashed past her. He caught Pierre up at the door of Dora's room.

Pierre was staring into the room. His eyes were as startled as the maid's. Dora lay, a crumpled heap, in the middle of the floor.

CHAPTER XIII

Gathering Darkness

"TAKE IT EASY," SAID HAZELDEAN QUIETLY, AS DORA OPENED her eyes.

He had lifted her into a chair after dismissing Pierre from the room. The old man had objected to the dismissal, but Hazeldean had not been in a mood to listen to his objections and had bundled him unceremoniously into the passage, closing the door in his indignant face. Possibly the face was now plastered to the keyhole, but Hazeldean did not mind the thought of that, since the key was in the hole on his side of the door, and in the event of further trouble he was quite ready to turn it.

Dora's eyes rested on him for a moment or two, during which the distress in them became less acute, and then they closed again. When next they opened, they remained open.

"Had a shock?" asked Hazeldean.

She nodded.

"Tell me about it when you're ready," he answered, "but don't hurry. We won't be interrupted," he added, as her glance wandered towards the door.

She waited a few moments longer, while the colour returned to her cheeks, then said.

"It was silly of me—to go off like that."

"Don't expect me to agree with you," he replied. "You seem to think everything you do is silly! There's a limit, you know, to what any of us can stand."

"Yes, I suppose so. Thank you. I expect it was—coming on top of everything—"

She paused and gulped, and now her glance wandered towards the window.

"What came on top of everything?" inquired Hazeldean. "Something at the window?"

"Yes."

"What?"

"A face. Dark—foreign." The brief description was sufficient for Hazeldean to recognise it. "It was only there for a moment."

"But it must have been a very nasty moment."

"Yes. And—you see—I'd still got that awful news you brought in my mind."

"Ah—your uncle told you about that?"

"Yes. He'd just gone. So I suppose the shock did it. Fainting isn't a habit of mine, though I do sometimes. It always annoys me. I never used to."

"Well, if you've grown into it, you'll grow out of it," he answered. "It's nothing to worry about. How are you feeling now?"

"Better," she replied, responding to his encouraging smile.

"How much better?"

"Quite all right."

"Do you need anything? Shall I ring for the maid?"

"Oh, no!" The negative was very definite. "Have you seen her? What do you think of her?"

"Of Marie?" he replied. "Well, she was quite pleasant while she served my tea. I can't say I was wildly enthusiastic, but I can't say I minded her."

"No. That's right." She was comparing her own opinion with his. "And what about Pierre? Have you seen him?"

"Yes."

"Are you wildly enthusiastic about Pierre?"

The form of the question pleased him. It was her first real attempt at humour, the invaluable tonic for jarred nerves.

"Do you remember a little rhyme about a certain Dr. Fell?" he asked.

"No."

"It goes like this: 'I do not like thee, Dr. Fell, the reason why I cannot tell, But this I know, and know full well, I do *not* like thee, Dr. Fell.'" Her laughter rippled round the dim parlour with pleasant incongruity. "So now you know my opinion of our friend Pierre. Incidentally, he hasn't got Marie's enterprise."

"What do you mean?"

"Well—Marie can speak a bit of English."

"Oh, but so can Pierre."

"Oh, can he?" Thus Hazeldean drew from Dora the information that Pierre had been lying, which further reduced the popularity of Dr. Fell. "My mistake. By the way, he hasn't been bothering you, has he?" She shook her head. "Or Marie? Was she here when you fainted?"

"No. I'd just had my meal." Her tray was still there. "You say you've had yours, or I'd—what are you going to do now?"

"Didn't your uncle tell you?" he asked.

"No."

"That's funny—"

"He was in a hurry," she explained. "He had to go to the police station with Madame Paula."

"Yes—of course... I'm staying here for a bit."

A pleasant moment followed. The spontaneous relief in her expression was ample repayment for his decision, though all she said was, "I'm glad!"

"Are you? Then so am I. It was your uncle who suggested it—"

"Did he?"

"But I expect I'd have suggested it myself if he hadn't. My man will be here shortly with some things from the boat."

She looked a little puzzled.

"But *didn't* you suggest it?" she asked. "I mean, when you left, wasn't Madame Paula going to show you a room?"

"So she was," he recalled.

"Only I wasn't sure you'd really decided."

"Well, I've decided now, anyhow. I'm in charge of you till he comes back. Do you mind?"

She smiled at him. "I like it. I hope it's a nice room. Some are very poky. I'll tell you something. I didn't think Madame Paula wanted it first—you to stay here, I mean. I had an idea she'd show you the horridest room there was, so you wouldn't take it! Yes, but now, of course, everything's different. Poor Madame Paula! I don't expect we'll be seeing much of her. My uncle said she'd be staying in her room." Her voice grew rather faltering. "Was I a little beast?"

"When?"

"I mean, the way I spoke about her. And about—I mean, when a thing like this happens, it makes you think. I wanted to go to her, but my uncle thought it was better not to."

"I'm sure he was right. And you weren't a little beast."

"Thank you. Only you would say that. I think I was, though. But, of course, I couldn't have seen her then, because they went out. I'm afraid it will be rather gloomy for you here. We don't do anything. Don't think you have to stay here and talk to me—if you want to go and see Notre Dame!"

She gave a nervous little laugh.

"I haven't the least desire to see Notre Dame!" he laughed back. "At least, not unless you come with me. But don't think you've got to talk to me either if *you* want to do anything else. Perhaps you want to get on with your book?"

The book she had been reading when he had first met her was on the little table by the tray.

"No, I'd much rather talk," she answered. "I don't often get the—I mean, I'm so afraid you'll find it dull, when I expect you meet so many interesting people—going about in your boat, and that. What shall we talk about?"

She was beginning suddenly to develop a painful self-consciousness, and though he longed to talk of personal matters, and meant to return to them, he decided to carry her mind away from herself and the pension and Boulogne for a little while. He described his boat to her, and his crew; and while the mantelpiece clock ticked away the minutes, and her interested face grew less and less distinct in the fading daylight, he took her on one of his voyages to Oslo and back. It was almost dark when he had finished.

"It must be a wonderful boat!" she exclaimed.

"It's just a boat," he replied. "But one's own boat is always wonderful, like one's dog or one's car."

"Could it go farther than Oslo and back?"

"Of course."

"Such a small boat?"

"She can sleep four comfortably. And she has an auxiliary engine."

"Could she go round the world?"

"Smaller boats have done it."

"It must be lovely to travel. To see things—new things. I wonder my uncle doesn't want to more sometimes. He came from South

Africa, you know. Well, of course, you didn't know. That was after my father died."

"When you were a little girl?"

"Well, fourteen or fifteen. I forget."

"You weren't fourteen when that picture of you was painted, were you?"

"Picture? Oh, in the dining-room at home? Yes, you've seen that, haven't you? There's something I still don't quite understand. Oh, well, never mind, I'm sure it doesn't really matter."

"What is it?"

"No, nothing. That picture. I was twelve."

"Then it was your father who commissioned it?"

"No, he painted it."

"Oh! He was an artist?"

"Only an amateur. I remember he used to tell me he couldn't paint for nuts. But he liked that picture. Another thing he told me was that it was the best thing he had ever done, and that really we'd both painted it, I was such a good sitter... We used to have great fun..."

Someone knocked on the door.

"Who is it? Entrez," called Dora.

The door opened, and Marie stood silhouetted against a faint light in the passage.

"Ze tray," she said, "et les drapeaux."

Hazeldean cursed her silently for her interruption, although he made use of it.

"I suppose no one's called to see me yet?" he asked as the maid crossed to the window and pulled the curtains.

It occurred to him that Bob Blythe should be arriving about now with his bag.

"Non, m'sieur," the maid answered.

"Please let me know the moment any one comes. Comprenez?"

"Mais oui!"

"Is Madame Paula back yet?"

"Oui, m'sieur."

"Comment elle portez vous?"

"Pardon?"

"How is she?"

"Ah! Je comprens! I 'ave not see 'er. She ees—lock in 'er room. Pierre me dit she is back and il faut zat she is not disturb."

She was leaving with the tray when Dora asked:

"Et Monsieur Fenner? A-t-il retourné?"

"Mais non, ma'm'selle. I fetch ze lamp."

When the door had closed and they were alone again, Hazeldean looked at Dora thoughtfully.

"Miss Fenner," he said, "please tell me something."

"Of course, if I can," she responded.

"You can. What was it you said you didn't understand just now—after I'd begun asking about the picture?"

She hesitated for a moment, then answered:

"Please don't mind—but I was wondering why you asked me all those questions about myself—and my movements yesterday."

"I—see," murmured Hazeldean slowly. "And you don't know?"

"But I don't mind. Really and truly! I'm sure you had a reason. And—and also for not telling me about Dr. Jones when I was talking about him."

Hazeldean got up, turned and stared towards the little clock on the mantelpiece. He was not especially interested in the clock, although time was beginning to have some significance, but he wanted to think for a few moments without Dora's inquiring eyes upon him.

"What's the matter?" came her voice, behind him.

"I'm just—working things out," he said. He turned round and faced her again. Each was a faint outline to the other, and would remain so till Marie returned with the lamp. "What did your uncle tell you?"

"What you told him."

"About—?"

"Dr. Jones."

"And, of course," said Hazeldean, after a little silence, "you couldn't understand the connection between all my questions and Dr. Jones?"

"No. Though—then—I *did* understand why you had left with Madame Paula."

"Let me see whether you understood that right."

"Wasn't it because you wanted to tell her alone? The room was just an excuse. That was why I decided afterwards that you mightn't really be staying on here—and—and why I was so glad when you said you were."

He nodded.

"All very good reasoning," he smiled, "whether you were right or wrong."

"Then wasn't I—?"

"Wait a moment, please. Now there's something I want you to tell *me* that *I* don't quite understand. Your last question to Marie."

"You mean about my uncle?"

"Yes. You asked whether he'd come back yet, too. Did you expect him back here to-night?"

She looked astonished.

"*Isn't* he coming back?" she exclaimed.

CHAPTER XIV

Marie

FROM BEYOND THE PARLOUR DOOR CAME THE SOUND OF FOOTsteps, and yellow light glowed and augmented in the crack. Before the door opened, thoughts raced through Hazeldean's mind in disorderly procession, tripping over each other's heels:

"He didn't tell her. He didn't tell her about the seven dead people at Haven House. She's no knowledge of this. She's sitting here, and she doesn't know. Why hasn't Bob turned up yet? I'll have to tell her. Shouldn't he be here? She thinks I called to give the news of Dr. Jones's accident. Why did Fenner let her think that? Why did he let her think he was going to return to-night? What did he tell Madame Paula? Where's the silk merchant? I suppose it *was* his face at the window. Marie is walking very quickly with the lamp. Still, she always does. Pierre. What about Pierre? He speaks English. Madame Paula's back, and in her room. We're not to disturb her. So Dora's father painted that picture. And they had fun. Does she have any fun with her uncle? South Africa. Aeroplane. Jones crashed. Dead cat. What was that about the dead cat? *Why* didn't Fenner tell her about seven dead people?…"

The door was open. Lamp-light entered the room. It re-developed objects that had faded, made shadows as it moved across the carpet, picked out the hands of Marie, who was grasping the lamp-pedestal. Marie's face, above the lamp-shade, looked like a little orange mist.

No one spoke. Was there any reason, in this fragment of ordinary domestic routine, why one should? Hazeldean studied the little orange mist, moving above the moving shadows. There was disturbance in it. It was not a serene mist. Why was Marie disturbed? Well, of course she was disturbed! Her master had been killed, and her mistress was locked in her room. Wasn't that enough to disturb anybody? But why was she more disturbed than she had been before—than when she had drawn the curtains and taken away the tray? Yes, and what was that scratch on the clearly illuminated right hand? The back of the hand. Had it been there before? Had Marie been a long time bringing in the lamp?

The scratch vanished as the lamp was placed on the little table where the tray had been and the hand was withdrawn.

"Have you had an accident?" asked Hazeldean.

"Pardon?" answered the maid. "Qu'est-ce c'est—accident?"

"Le meme en Français, n'est-ce pas? Accident?"

"Ah! Accident!" repeated Marie, while Hazeldean thought: "This is Pierre's trick—she understood the first time! 'Mais non!'"

"Votre main?" he insisted.

She looked at her hand.

"Oh, cela! C'est rien!" Avoiding Hazeldean's sceptical eye, she transferred her gaze to Dora and explained, "I break ze cup."

The next instant she had gone.

"Something's the matter, isn't it?" said Dora.

"I'm not sure," he replied.

"Aren't you? I am. You'll have to trust me in the end, you know."

"Trust you? Of course I trust you!"

"I mean—with anything I don't yet know. I suppose you're thinking I can't stand it?"

"I'm sure you'll stand anything you have to," he answered, while her eyes searched his.

"Then please tell me why my uncle told me he was returning to-night, when *you* know that he wasn't?"

"I'll tell you that, Miss Fenner, when I know it myself. Will you stay here for a few minutes till I come back?"

"You want to ask Marie some more questions?"

"Yes."

"I could ring for her."

"I'd rather go after her."

"Mr. Hazeldean," said Dora, "you've seen me faint. That won't happen again. But do you want to hear me scream?" Then she smiled a little wearily. "I'm sorry. I didn't mean that. Go after Marie."

He had been hovering near the door. Now he left the door and went to her. She looked up at him from her chair with a pathetic attempt to conceal her apprehension.

"Listen, Miss Fenner," he said. "If I'm not handling this as well as I ought to—if I'm bungling a bit—I know you'll forgive me. But I do understand what you're going through, and if you screamed, I wouldn't blame you in the least! Only you're not going to scream. I *am* going to trust you shortly with something you don't know—that will end your indecision. But until just now I thought you already knew it. I thought your uncle had told you—"

"You mean, there *was* something besides Dr. Jones's accident?"

"Of course. Something that will explain all my questions to you. As a matter of fact—" He hesitated, then went on: "As a matter of fact, I didn't bring the news about Dr. Jones at all. I didn't know it. It was your uncle who brought that. I'm sure, when we've got to the bottom of this, we'll find that he had some good reason for giving you a wrong impression."

"Oh, no, you don't think that!" she retorted, with a sudden shrewdness that surprised him.

"Why don't I?" he asked.

"Because, if you thought it was a good reason, you'd leave him to work it out. Wouldn't you? But now you're going to tell me what *he* wouldn't!"

"Your point," he smiled. "Just the same, I'm not going to blame your uncle for anything until I've got my facts—and perhaps it would be a good idea if you didn't, either."

"Perhaps," she replied, and then surprised him again by adding, with the nearest approach to venom of which he imagined she was capable: "And perhaps *not*!… Well, please go now. I'll wait here, I promise. And the sooner you go, the sooner you'll be back, and—and tell me."

Then he left her.

Along the passage he heard whispering. When he got round the angle from beyond which the whispering had sounded, he saw no one. Another angle and a few stairs took him into the front hall. Marie was standing by a chair, intently dusting it.

"Do you do your dusting so late in the day?" asked Hazeldean.

She turned swiftly, but had no reply.

"And with your mouchoir?" he added. Still nothing came into an apparently blank mind. "How did you *really* get that scratch?"

He pointed to her injured hand.

"Ze cup," she answered, parrot-fashion.

"Merci. And maintenant, s'il vous plait, la vérité?"

"Pardon!"

Her indignation was unconvincing.

"Oui, Marie. La vérité, toute la vérité, et rien que la vérité! Si ce n'est pas juste, vous me comprenez!"

"C'est juste," she muttered, no longer attempting the indignation. She glanced towards a curtain. The curtain led to the passage along which Madame Paula had conducted him on their way to the attic.

"Well? Will you tell it to me, or shall I ask Pierre—or Madame Paula?"

"Madame Paula!" exclaimed Marie. "She is lock in 'er chambre!"

"So I understand. But Pierre is not lock in his chambre."

"'E will not tell eet to you!"

The next instant she looked startled as she realised the implication of her remark.

"Then there is something to tell?" he insisted. "And Pierre knows what it is."

"'E will not tell."

"Then I shall have to ask Madame Paula—"

"Mais oui! Ca sera bien simple! Pierre will not stop you, oh, no!"

The words came in a sudden fierce flurry, and now her indignation was genuine enough. Only it was not directed this time against Hazeldean.

"I see," he murmured.

"Quoi donc?"

"You got your scratch from Pierre. Well, you can at least tell me about *that*." She glanced again towards the curtained passage. "Attendez, Marie. You and Pierre were whispering—parlering—as I came along just now. Then Pierre left you quickly—through that curtain, eh?—and you pretended to be busy dusting a chair with your mouchoir. Do you comprener what I'm saying?"

She nodded sullenly.

"Well, am I right?"

"Oui, m'sieur."

She had become submissive as well as sullen. Hazeldean realised that he had won a psychological battle, and he made the most of it.

"Why did Pierre go away so quickly?"

"He hear you coming."

"Yes, but why should that trouble him?"

"I do not know zat."

"What were you talking about?"

"Il me demande—'e ask me what 'appen."

"In the parlour? Miss Fenner's room?"

"Oui, m'sieur."

"And you told him?"

"No."

"Why not? Nothing particular happened, did it?"

"I say, 'Ces questions, pourquoi?'"

"You weren't on good terms with him?"

"Good term? Je ne comprends pas."

"Vous ne l'aimez pas?"

"Aujourd'hui, non!"

Her tone was emphatic.

"Because of your quarrel?"

She looked at him, then followed his gaze down to her scratched hand.

"Oui."

"What was the quarrel about? Pourquoi quarrelez-vous?"

"Eet is about Madame Paula."

"Well?"

"I am—je suis désolé. Triste. La pauvre!" She frowned, as though not quite understanding herself. "She is not toujours so good to me, non, mais—domage! Aujourd'hui! Aujourd'hui! So I go to 'er door; but Pierre is zere, and 'e say, 'Non!' 'Per'aps she need somesing,' I say. 'Ze lamp.' But 'e say, 'Allez, allez, she is not to be disturb, I 'ave ze ordaire, allez!' And when I spik encore, mon Dieu, 'e go red and 'e say, 'Taisez-vous, taisez-vous!' To 'old ze tongue!"

She paused, breathlessly. Her slow, unwilling mind had suddenly accelerated in a tide of anger. Hazeldean took advantage of the pause to ask:

"Was this when you went for the lamp for Miss Fenner?"

"Oui," answered Marie. "It make me sink of ze lamp for Madame, aussi."

"Did you have to obey Pierre?"

"Mais non! And I tell 'im! But when I go to ze door 'e get in my way, and when I slap 'is face, oui, 'e bite me; zen I bite 'im, and we 'ave, qu'est-ce que c'est?—le fisticuff!"

"And Pierre won?" asked Hazeldean, unable to suppress a smile. But Marie frowned as she nodded. "Thank you, Marie. Thank you very much. Well, if I want to see Madame Paula, I don't suppose Pierre will try any fisticuffs on *me*. I think it was very nice of you to try to do something for Madame Paula. You like thinking of others, don't you?" Marie looked a little puzzled, though whether at the words or the compliment, he was not sure. "You like helping people?"

"Mais oui, m'sieur," she replied, divided between pleasure and suspicion. Now that her outburst was over, her personal anxiety seemed to be hovering back.

"Would you like to help Mademoiselle Fenner?"

The maid stared at him hard, then suddenly smiled rather mystically. "Ah, la pauvre!" she murmured, and tapped her forehead.

"Who the devil told—qui a dit cela?" he demanded.

Now Marie's heavy eyebrows shot up.

"N'est-ce vrai?" she asked.

"Of course it's not vrai!" he retorted. "Je pense que c'est vrai de autre—des autres—oh, blazes! Anyhow, voulez-vous aller to Mademoiselle Fenner, and stay avec elle jusque je retourne? Dites-elle que j'ai le demandé."

The maid's eyebrows remained up, with fresh astonishment.

"Marie," said Hazeldean, "êtes-vous satisfé avec toutes les choses dans ce maison?"

"Cette," murmured Marie. "Non!"

"Moi aussi non. Ainsi, voulez-vous?"

"Oui! Oui! Je comprends!"

"Merci! Et maintenant, s'il-vous plait. Vitement!"

She turned at once and left him. Relieved that Dora would now have someone with her should trouble occur during the next few minutes, he moved towards the curtain, then paused.

"Oh, Marie!" he called softly over his shoulder just before she disappeared. "Qu'est-ce que c'est le nombre de la chambre de Madame Paula?"

"Numero Deux," she replied. "Prenez garde!"

"I mean to pren beaucoup de garde," he smiled, and went through the curtain.

CHAPTER XV

Numero Deux

PIERRE WAS STANDING OUTSIDE NUMERO DEUX WHEN Hazeldean approached the door, and he gave no sign of any intention to move. Even when Hazeldean stopped, the old man remained motionless, apparently staring into space.

"S'il vous plait?" said Hazeldean.

Pierre's only response was to shorten his focus vaguely and to raise his shaggy eyebrows.

"I spoke distinctly," remarked Hazeldean, "and I spoke in French. But you're understanding me just as well this time, aren't you?"

"Pardon?" frowned the old man.

"You're wasting time," retorted Hazeldean. "You and I have several things to clear up in due course, but we'll clear up one of them now. Why have you been pretending not to understand English?"

Doggedly Pierre continued the pretence.

"And—while we're at it—why are you guarding that door so solicitously when you know, as well as I do, that Madame Paula is in the dining-room with a policeman?"

Pierre opened his mouth, then closed it quickly, but not quite quickly enough. The little ruse had succeeded.

"You're not even a clever rascal," said Hazeldean contemptuously. "Get out of my way."

"Pourquoi?" growled the old man.

"Did you hear me?"

"Mais—si Madame est dans la salle a manger—avec le gendarme—?"

The words were spat out, malicious in their admission.

"Quite so. But, as you already know, she isn't in the dining-room, and there is no gendarme here—yet! Now will you move?"

The old man gave a surly shrug and stayed where he was.

"Or must I make you?"

The old man's eyes became watchful.

"Well, if I hurt you it'll be your fault," said Hazeldean. "It doesn't amuse me to be rough with white hairs. For the last time of asking, will you get out of my way?"

Pierre's reply was swift and unexpected. Adopting the axiom that attack is the surest means of defence, and with every reason to assume that defence was going to be necessary, he shot out a bony fist and caught Hazeldean on the chin.

"Some blow, for eighty!" muttered Hazeldean. "Is that a wig you're wearing?"

"Allez, allez!" rasped Pierre.

"Sorry, but now you're going to get hit yourself. Don't say I haven't warned you. One, two, three, bang!"

The warning was a mistake. Pierre ducked, and his long, lean arms wound themselves round Hazeldean's body. In the next few seconds an Englishman had a taste of a Frenchman's method of fighting. Teeth, nails, feet—everything was utilised, and with a strength and skill that added the element of surprise. Whatever Pierre's age, he was a very long way from falling to bits. He fought like a tiger.

But Hazeldean, once he found half-measures fruitless, gauged Pierre's strength and learned his tricks. One trick had tripped him to the ground; but they had fallen together, and they began rolling along the passage. This, Hazeldean discovered, was another trick, for the passage led to a steep flight of stairs down which there could be a very nasty accident. Managing to pull up on the brink, he twisted his adversary round and sat on top of him.

"Whew! That's that!" panted Hazeldean. "Only I think, before we part company, I'd like your keys."

The old man glared speechlessly. His strength seemed spent.

"You see," continued Hazeldean, groping for his pockets, "you *may* have the key to Numero Deux, and I don't want to have to come back for it."

He found a bunch of keys and one separate one. He took the lot. Then, rising from Pierre's chest, he walked back to the door of Madame Paula's room.

"Madame must be sleeping very soundly if *that* row didn't wake her up!" he thought.

He knocked on the door—softly at first, then more loudly. Madame Paula gave no sign of having heard.

"Of course, she may have taken a sleeping draught," he reflected, giving every possibility its chance.

He glanced back along the passage. Pierre had managed to rise to his knees, whimpering. He glared back at Hazeldean, on all fours like a whipped and sulky dog. His immediate need seemed to be the comfort of an adjacent chair.

"Well, now for it," decided Hazeldean.

He tried the separate key and found that it fitted. He turned it, and a substantial lock left its socket with a click. He turned the door-knob and softly pushed the door open.

"My God!" he murmured.

A figure lay stretched on the bed. But it was not the figure of Madame Paula. It was the dark-skinned vendor of coloured silks.

The next moment something descended with a crash on his head.

CHAPTER XVI

Meanwhile, at Benwick…

DETECTIVE-INSPECTOR KENDALL RETURNED SLOWLY THROUGH the little wood. He was feeling rather pleased with himself, a frame of mind which he did not often allow. Professionally, he was an enemy of over-confidence; and privately, he loathed conceit. But he was to cross to Boulogne on the late afternoon boat in his effort to trace the Fenners, and he chuckled as he dwelt on the neat manner in which, he hoped, he had sent an advance guard. "That pleasant young fool has fallen in love with the picture of a little girl," he reflected, "and his one object now is to meet the big girl. Well, I hope he does. Heart sometimes succeeds where art lags behind!"

This was why he walked slowly, and even stopped and turned back. When, emerging from the wood, he glimpsed the creek, and he saw the *Spray* moving out of it. He chuckled again, turned once more and re-entered the wood.

That being that, his busy mind moved to another point.

"Seven people, whether dead or alive, cannot be in a house without having got there," he thought, "unless, of course, they were born there and stayed put. Which is unlikely. How did these seven people get to Haven House? Through this wood, obviously. There are not sufficient marks in the road at the front, and the few marks there are are not the right marks. Here there are plenty of marks—here and in the muddy bank of the creek—and our two measured sets of prints fit the boots of two of the seven people. We may temporarily assume the rest. But how did they arrive at the creek? By boat, obviously. There are some new scratches and rubbings against the edge of the landing-stage. But where is the boat? Did someone bring them and then go away again? If so, I must find that someone. If not... Kendall, there's a hell of a lot to do."

The trees thinned. Just ahead was the beginning of the garden lawn. Just off the path was a little black, silky heap.

"And how did that cat die?" mused Kendall, pausing. "Is this—Number Eight?"

He bent down and examined the animal. He sniffed. He sniffed again, closer. "Dr. Saunders," he murmured as he straightened himself. "I think you must see this cat!"

He looked across the lawn, visualising a cat's course from the house and regretting there was no way of proving the picture. The lawn's occupants at the moment were Sergeant Wade, a constable and a thin young man with a note-book. The sergeant was thoroughly enjoying a good excuse for an officious mood. "I can't help about your public, I've got mine," came his stern voice. "And orders are orders! There's a man on the gate, he can take a message; and we can't have no climbing through hedges—not if you was the Editor of the *Times*!" Kendall smiled and, catching the constable's eye, beckoned to him.

"Stand by this cat," he instructed the constable, when the man drew up; "and if anybody tries to touch it, tick 'em off as the sergeant's ticking off that journalist."

The constable grinned, then stared at the cat.

"Dead, ain't it?" he said.

"You surprise me," answered Kendall.

On the point of crossing the lawn, he suddenly glanced along the edge of the wood and paused.

"Constable," he said. "Do cats move round in circles, like dogs and politicians?"

"Dogs do," replied the constable.

"You're behind the times," remarked Kendall. "I've already implied that fact."

Instead of crossing the lawn, he moved to examine a little nest of grass. Then he gazed beyond and followed a new course between trees, studying the ground carefully as he walked. The cat might have disturbed the grass, but human feet had worn the track he was now pursuing.

The track began along the edge of the wood. Then it turned inwards, away from the house, winding and zigzagging between bushes. It ended in a big tangle of undergrowth.

Kendall sniffed. He brought out an electric torch and played it into the tangle. "Someone's closed the front door!" he murmured. "Why? And what's beyond the front door?"

He parted some branches, most, though not all, of which appeared to have been recently introduced. Forcing his way through, he found himself in a short, narrow tunnel of twigs and leaves and creepers. He sniffed again, made a grimace, brought out his handkerchief with difficulty, wiped his forehead, blew his nose, and played his torch down a large hole. Gingerly he let himself into the hole. He dropped on to earth. Ahead, his torch glowed on a long cavity fitted with shelves.

"A.R.P.?" he murmured sceptically.

There were other things besides shelves. A bench, a stool, rubber tubing, a pail, empty bottles, indecipherable oddments, and a considerable quantity of broken glass. Also, another dead cat.

He lingered in the underground cell for just as long as was necessary, which was also just as long as he could stand, and then escaped back into the air, taking a bit of the rubber tubing with him. On his way out he noticed two more things. One was a substantial slab of wood about a yard square; this was near the entrance to the hole, and its area was sufficient to cover the hole comfortably. The second, which he pocketed, was a fragment of grey cloth caught on a twig.

He found the constable still guarding the cat. Sergeant Wade had joined him, and was airing his views.

"That cat never died natural," declared the sergeant.

"'Ow do you make that out?" asked the constable.

"Because," replied Wade, "a cat that dies natural don't look like that."

"What does a cat look like, Wade," inquired Kendall, as he drew up, "when it dies natural?"

"Not like that," insisted the sergeant.

"Well, what did this cat die of?"

"Ah, there you are!"

"It died of a complaint similar to that which killed seven people in a drawing-room. Come along, stop staring, and let's get back to the house. Carry on, constable. Anything new, Wade, while I've been away?"

"They're still trying to find that old forwarding address at the post office," replied the sergeant, falling into step. "Died the same way as the others did it?"

"It's a confounded nuisance they can't trace the re-direction form."

"I've told 'em they've got to. See, if it had been filled in more than once they might have remembered it—but a year ago—and they don't think there was anything to forward, even then."

"What happens to the Fenners' mail ordinarily when they're away?"

"I expect it stays. Waits for 'em."

"Queer they don't always have it forwarded, isn't it?"

"Well, they aren't often away for very long; and they get very little, anyhow. So the postman says. Oh, yes, I forgot. There was a letter came yesterday morning with a French stamp."

"Yesterday morning?" exclaimed Kendall. "Why the devil didn't you tell me before?"

"Well, I'm telling you now, sir."

"By which post?"

"First post. Early morning."

"Anybody notice the postmark?"

"Boulogne."

"Wade, do you know who killed those seven people?"

"Eh? No, sir!"

"I only thought you might have forgotten to mention it! We're trying to find a man, we learn that a letter from Boulogne is delivered to him shortly before he vanishes, and you bring it in casually with the weather. Well, what else? Those descriptions. Have they been circulated? All seven?"

"Yes, sir."

"Photographs?"

"Being rushed, sir."

"Black looking after that?"

"Yes, sir."

"I suppose nobody's come forward yet to identify anybody?"

"No. Not since you left, sir."

"Had anybody come forward before?"

"No, sir."

"Then why use six words? Two would have done. Any inquiries? Of any kind?"

"No, sir."

"Aeroplane?"

"Fixed up, sir."

"Let's hear."

"They came through quarter of an hour ago. Start at 3.30. That'll get you in Folkestone in time for the boat." The sergeant paused, then added: "Why don't you go all the way by air?"

"And miss the *Isle of Thanet*? No, thank you. Once I'm at Folkestone by air, the rest won't take much longer by sea, and I'm interested in that voyage. Also, I'm meeting someone at the other side. Fingerprints?"

"You could paper a wall with 'em."

"Quite an idea for a detective's study. Whorl-paper, eh?" He stopped as they reached the french windows. "Something damnable about those shutters, Wade. Not merely closed, but nailed. *Nailed*. Shutters nailed, and chimney stuffed up... And there are some people who don't believe in capital punishment!... Well, p'r'aps they're right. Ever seen a man swing, Wade?... That cricket ball intrigues me. Funny colour, isn't it? Yes, there's no doubt about it, we've got a puzzle on; but we're moving, and we'll unearth some devil or other before we're through. Come along. Revolver. Whose fingerprints were on that?"

"The old man's, sir," answered the sergeant as they moved again and stepped off grass on to gravel.

"Ah! Then he *did* fire it!"

"Unless someone else pressed his fingers on the thing afterwards."

"Improving, Wade. You'll get promotion yet. Only I don't think that's really what happened this time. Here we are—back at the House of the Dead. Come into the hall, and I'll show what *I* think happened."

They had reached the front porch, and he darted in. Wade followed more slowly, to find the detective opening the drawing-room door.

"We'll have the dining-room door open, too," called Kendall, "because at the moment I'm going to reconstruct I'll wager anything you like it wasn't closed. Open it, will you? A bit more. Whoa! I think that'll do. Now, then!"

He stood for a moment, staring across the hall towards the dining-room door. Then he transferred his gaze to the sergeant, who fought an uncomfortable impression that something unpleasant was coming.

"In a moment," said Kendall, "I want you to imagine I am the old man who—we are assuming—fired that shot. You yourself are an unknown individual called X, and your object is to lock me in the drawing-room with my six companions. Wait a bit. What is my condition? Am I hale and hearty—that is to say, as hale and hearty as my wasted condition will allow—or am I already drifting off?" He ceased speaking for an instant and closed his eyes. "I don't know, Wade," he went on, opening them again. "I don't know. But I've still got enough strength and spunk to pull a trigger. Yes, and—afterwards—to write… Well, let's get on. Lock the door, and if I try to interfere, damn' well see I don't. Be as rough as you like—and, I warn you, look out for yourself. Though, of course, any subsequent doctor's bills will be debited in the official accounts. Au revoir, Wade."

He vanished inside the drawing-room. The sergeant paused for an instant to swallow. He was not quite sure that he fully appreciated this new form of instruction. It was a bit too vivid, and stirred uncomfortably his usually unimaginative mind. He almost felt as though he *were* the unidentified X, and as though the old, grey-haired gentleman had actually come to life in there—with his six companions—and were really going to reproduce one of the gruesome events of yesterday! "I'll see I lock that door!" thought Wade suddenly. "Yes, and if there's any interference, and he *wants* it, he shall *have* it!"

He dived to the door. As he did so, Kendall came rushing out. He looked wild.

"Hey, back you go!" shouted Wade, while the spirit of X seemed to swoop inside him. Perhaps it did. Not many hours had elapsed to wipe it out.

The next moment the sergeant ducked. Kendall's hand had shot out.

"Bang!" bawled Kendall over Wade's head.

Wade's head buffeted into Kendall's stomach. With queer satisfaction the sergeant saw, or rather felt, his superior totter back into the room.

"Bang!" he bawled back.

And slammed and locked the door.

After a second or two Kendall's voice came through the wood. It was quiet now, though it bore an amused, almost mocking note.

"Coming in?"

"No, thanks," muttered Wade, now feeling a little ashamed of himself for his over-acting.

"Why not?"

"P'r'aps I shan't be so lucky next time!"

"Exactly. I missed you, didn't I? As you say, next time you might be less fortunate, and I might hit you. You see, I've still got this revolver, and you've no need to press my fingers on the barrel. Unlock the door now, Wade, and let's see where my bullet went. All quiet on the Western Front."

Wade unlocked the door. Kendall smiled at him, then looked beyond his shoulder. Wade turned, following his gaze.

"Out of the drawing-room, over your head across the hall, into the dining-room, and across to the picture. Follow the line? *That's* what happened, Wade. That's what happened… Yes. Yes… But—afterwards?"

Sergeant Wade mopped his brow.

"Yes—what happened afterwards?" he muttered.

Kendall did not reply. He was looking very thoughtful, and there was a little extra colour on his usually uninformative cheeks. He turned back to the drawing-room door, closed it and re-locked it. Then he removed the key. Then he took a length of thin rubber tubing from his pocket and, after squinting through the keyhole, inserted an end of the tubing in the hole.

"Just fits—doesn't it?" he murmured. "Of course, there was something more on this end."

It seemed to the sergeant that he held the tubing in the keyhole for a full minute. Then he withdrew the tubing and replaced the key.

"And all we've got to do now, Wade," he said, "is to find the man and the motive."

CHAPTER XVII

Exit a Bicycle and Enter a Boat

WHILE DETECTIVE-INSPECTOR KENDALL HAD A BUSY PERIOD with the telephone in the hall, Sergeant Wade made another tour of the grounds, returning just as Kendall replaced the receiver for the last time.

"Well?" asked Kendall.

"I've had a look at that dug-out," answered Wade, "and I ain't making no offers for it!"

"Didn't like the smell?"

"Filthy."

"But you recognised it?" The sergeant nodded. "What's your opinion?"

"Same as yours, sir. Sort of a—underground workshop, eh?"

"With some of the original contents removed."

"That's right."

"What I'd like to find," said Kendall, "is whatever fitted on to that tubing."

"Maybe he wouldn't leave it around," replied the sergeant.

"He? Who?"

"X," smiled the sergeant. "That's me, ain't it?"

Kendall smiled back.

"I think you're right. X wouldn't leave it around. He's probably left more around than he meant, as it is—but you can't think of everything when your first thought is your own skin. I've phoned up the doctor, and I've suggested that he gets in touch with your local Decontamination Squad. He's coming along with the foreman to have a look at our funk-hole. Also, the cats. But, of course, Saunders already knew death was due to some form of gas, only he doesn't know what form. I've a notion the form is going to be more important than he seems to think himself. I've suggested the Home Office as a further reference. You might keep 'em up to that if they get in a tangle and I'm not around."

The sergeant reacted pleasantly to the subtle flattery. *He'd* keep 'em up to it!

"But aren't you going to be around?" he asked.

"I'm off to Boulogne at 3.30," Kendall reminded him, "and I've a lot to do before that."

"Did you get on to Boulogne just now, sir?"

"Yes."

"Fix it up?"

"That's all O.K."

The next question came after a moment's hesitation.

"Have you thought about the Yard, sir?"

"I see *you* have."

"Well, yes, sir," admitted the sergeant. "Seven's a bit of a handful—"

"And too many cooks spoil the broth," interposed Kendall. "Don't you think you and I and Black and Saunders can handle this?" He smiled. "Make your mind easy about that, Wade. I'm in touch with the Yard—so's the Chief—that was another of my phone calls—and they'll send someone along the moment we need 'em. We may need 'em if I'm detained in Boulogne, though Black's a good man. *He* doesn't play the violin, either, or quote Shakespeare. By the way, what's *your* instrument?"

"Eh?"

"All the best people have a hobby, sergeant."

"Oh! I get you. Darts."

"Capital. Now, then. Listen. I've a job for you. Black's got his hands full, and anyway as you're the local man this is up your street. I want the complete history of John Fenner. All you know about him and all you can find out. His habits; his character; his work; his movements; how long he's been living in Benwick; when he came here; if he wasn't born here, where did he come from? Never mind if some of it's repetition. Write the whole damn' thing out from A to Z, and pack in all the details you can. You can even mention his tooth-paste, if you like. But what I'd rather you mentioned than anything else," he added, "is how Fenner left Benwick yesterday, since he doesn't seem to have gone by train, and the absence of a garage suggests he hasn't a car."

"That's right, there's no garage here," nodded the sergeant. "But there's a shed, and his bicycle's gone."

Kendall stared at him.

"There are moments," he said, "when you come out with the most interesting remarks."

"Well, sir, didn't you notice the bicycle was gone?" asked the sergeant.

"How could I have noticed it was gone," answered Kendall, "when I didn't know it had ever been there?"

"Ah, I get you."

"So Fenner rides a bicycle?"

"I seen him on it often."

"Lately?"

"Couple of days ago."

"What kind?"

"Hercules."

"How do you know?"

"Eh?"

"What made you notice it? Have you had anything to do with it? Do you notice the make of every bicycle you see? If so, you shouldn't be a sergeant in Benwick. You should be one of the Big Five."

"Ah, I get you. Well, see, he come in the bicycle shop last Thursday, when I happen to be there."

"Rather an attractive girl in the bicycle shop, isn't there?"

"Eh?"

"Do you mind saying 'Eh?' a little less often, Wade?"

"Well, I don't suppose he went in to see *her*."

"That wasn't precisely my thought," answered Kendall dryly, as he got up. "Come along, we'll look at that shed where there was once a bicycle." As they left the house he went on: "What *did* he go in the bicycle shop for?"

"To have a puncture mended."

"And was it mended?"

"Eh? I mean, what?"

"I asked you, sergeant, whether the puncture was mended."

"I know you did, sir," the sergeant fought back. "But, even if I was one o' the Big Five, how'd I know that?"

"Meaning you don't know that?"

"No."

"So the reason the bicycle isn't in the shed may be because it is still at the shop?"

Wade looked crestfallen, but he wasn't quite beaten yet.

"What I do wrong, sir," he said, "is to mention things. I get you."

Sarcasm was met by sarcasm.

"If you got me as often as you think you do, I should be in a permanent state of capture," answered Kendall. They were emerging from the narrow path by the side of the house on to the back lawn. "Your trouble isn't that you fail to mention things, Wade, but that you mention them too late, and then incompletely. I have no doubt that, three years after your death, you will send somebody the information. Listen—and with your mind this time, not your mouth. A bicycle is missing from a shed. It may be vital. Yet you only refer to it as a comment on a casual remark of my own. You don't come to me and say, 'Bicycle missing from shed, sir—Fenner's.' And even then, when the information is forced out of you by accident, you make no attempt to give it its proper value. Again it has to be forced out of you that the bicycle *may* be missing from the shed because it is at a cycle shop. This is what you should have reported to me, Wade, without any prompting: 'Bicycle missing from shed, sir—Fenner's. Two days ago he took it to have a puncture mended, so it may be at the shop; but it ought to be back by now. It's a Hercules. Model C. Rubber pedals, roller lever brakes front and rear, spring seat, black enamel without lining—speaking now of the finish, sir, not the seat—and Dunlop Sports tyres. The reason I mention the tyres, sir, is because p'r'aps we can trace 'em from the shed. Oh, and by the way, sir, that's a damn' smart little filly serving in the shop, isn't she?'"

"Yes, she is," answered Wade, giving up.

The shed was at the side of the back lawn, halfway across. Kendall lifted his eyes from the ground as they reached the rotting door and shoved it open. He glanced round swiftly, noted the wooden shelf and few oddments around, and inquired:

"How do you know he kept his bicycle here?"

"I don't," replied the sergeant guardedly. "But where else would he keep it?"

"That's good enough," said Kendall, "when you add the oil-mark on the floor and that small spanner."

"Where's the lamp the oil came from?" asked the sergeant.

"Probably on the bicycle," suggested Kendall. "But why an oil-lamp, when an electric one is so much more convenient?"

"Well, there you are. But he uses an oil lamp."

"Oh, you know that?"

"I heard him telling her to fill it."

"She seems to have over-filled it."

They left the shed, and Kendall studied the ground. A narrow, worn strip stretched to the wood and turned along it just before reaching the trees. Before the turn the ground was hard; after, it became softer, with patches of mud and sand. "Dunlop, his mark," murmured Kendall. "Come along, Wade! This mark's been made since last Thursday."

"You mean that rain on Thursday night?"

"Yes. The mud might have held it, but the sand wouldn't. I believe we're getting somewhere."

They followed the tyre marks. The marks continued outside the little wood till the trees ended, then ran across an indeterminate space to the bank of the creek, reaching it at a spot considerably farther from the mouth than the landing-stage. They continued along the bank.

After about fifty yards, a gap in a low hedge led to a lane. The gap was at a corner. One way still clung to the river bank, the other went inland. The tyre marks remained faithful to the river.

"Where does the other way go?" asked Kendall. "To the road that leads to the front of the house?"

"That's right," answered Wade.

"Bring the car round. Quick as you know how. I'll wait for you here."

The sergeant nodded and trotted off. He was quite ready to give his brain ten minutes' rest. Kendall watched his portly back till it vanished round a curve, then turned and looked down at the water.

At first the detective's eyes were moody. He was not thinking of the water, but of the track along the lane beside it. He wanted to follow the track until he had unearthed the bicycle that had made it, and it was because he believed the track would prove a long one that he had sent for the car. But all at once he forgot the track, and his eyes paid attention to the water. A small motor-boat had chugged round a bend from the direction of the creek mouth.

The motor-boat by itself would not have interested Kendall. Motor-boats were as natural to a river as ploughs to a farm. It was on the ancient craft behind that his eyes became glued—an old boat with an old mast, decrepit with service, and giving the impression that it was being towed home to die, saving that it had obviously never been born on the Essex coast. If the head of the procession was indigenous, the tail was exotic.

"Looks as old as that cricket ball," thought Kendall. "Why the devil am I comparing it with the cricket ball?"

And then a strange thing happened, although it merely happened in Kendall's mind. The towed boat was empty, yet he saw seven people in it—seven people moving towards their death in a boat already dead...

"Hey!" he shouted to the man in the motor-boat—an old salt smoking a pipe.

The old salt took the pipe out of his mouth.

"Can you draw in?" called the detective. "I want to speak to you."

"Wh'about?" bawled the old salt.

"That Noah's Ark you're towing," replied Kendall. "Where did you pick it up?"

The old salt waved to a spot a little way along the bank and altered his course towards it. Kendall made for the spot, scrambling down to water level just as the boat drew up.

"Where did you find that ocean liner?" he repeated.

"'Oo?" blinked the old salt.

"That boat. Did you fish it up on a hook?"

"Oh! Noa! She wer' floatin' by 'ersel', so I've brought 'er along."

"Derelict, eh?"

"Noa! She wer' floatin' by 'ersel', so I've brought 'er along."

"So I gather. May I step aboard and have a look at her?"

"Be she your'n?"

"No, but I may be able to tell you something about her. Where did you spot her?"

"South o' Maplin Spit. Nigh West Mouse."

"I'm afraid I don't know your map. Where are those places?"

"West Swin, off Maplin Sands."

Kendall swore under his breath.

"Your name's James Jessop, isn't it?" he asked.

"Ay, ev'ryone knows Jessop," answered the old salt.

"Well, Jessop, a few people know Detective-Inspector Kendall, so kindly attend to him. Stop being local and speak common, everyday English. How far were you from the coast when you saw this boat?"

"She wer' floatin' be 'ersel'—"

"And you brought her along. How many miles did you bring her?"

"Oh, I see. Well, sir, might be fower."

"Four miles. Could she have floated those four miles from the mouth of this river?"

"I never thought o' that."

"No, Jessop, I'm thinking of it. Could she? You know the tides?"

"I doen't see why not."

"If, say, she'd been in the river mouth some time—yesterday afternoon or evening?"

"I doen't see why not."

"Winds and tides right for it?"

"Ay, it could be. But there wu'n't much wind till mist cleared."

"And could this be, Jessop? You see that mooring rope?"

"Ay, what there be of it."

"Exactly. Perhaps not long ago there was more of it. Perhaps it was tied to a post nearer the mouth of this river. The rope that remains is old and rotted—and frayed. I see *you're* not depending on it!"

"'Oo would, in senses?"

"You've hit the nail again, Jessop! Out of the mouths of babes and sucklings... As you say, who would, in their senses? Yes, but tell me this, Jessop. Would you be in your senses if you were about to commit suicide?"

"Eh?"

"Still, I'm not banking on that. What I'm banking on is another kind of agitation—and at this moment I'm damned if I know what that is any more than you do!"

The old salt scratched his head.

"Beggin' yer pardon, sir, but be *you* out o' your senses?"

"You didn't hit the nail quite so well that time," smiled Kendall. "Still, I don't blame you. Now we won't talk for a bit. I want to examine this old tub."

"But I got to report it," said Jessop.

"You're reporting it to me," returned Kendall. "I'm the police."

While the old man re-lit his pipe and watched him, the detective explored the towed boat thoroughly. It had oars and a sail. The sail was in tatters. It was amply provided with lockers. In one he found half a biscuit. A dog in full strength might have managed it. In another he found fishing tackle. In another, a number of empty bottles, a big water-cask and a small piece of pasteboard. The piece of pasteboard had slipped down a crack, and he had to dig it out.

He examined it minutely. Particularly one side. It seemed to have been through every kind of experience, like the boat itself and the old cricket ball. Kendall could never get that cricket ball out of his mind. It had been drowned, palpably, several times. As he slipped it in his pocket his eyes were grim.

He made one more important discovery, the fruit of an obvious search. Faintly against the rubbed outside of the boat were the letters:

F RND LE

He was staring at the letters, and at the empty spaces after the first and the fourth, when a car loomed above him on the bank, and Sergeant Wade's voice descended:

"Thought I'd lost you, sir. What have we got here?"

"The boat seven people arrived at Benwick in," answered Kendall.

"What!" cried the sergeant.

"The name of the boat is probably *Ferndale*," continued Kendall, "and it doesn't look to me like an English boat, though the name's English enough. I should say it's off some ship. It's designed to carry plenty of provisions, and there's a water-cask. Still, of course… Well, what do you say?"

"Same as you, sir," replied the sergeant, staring at the boat. "Been through a bit, eh?"

"I imagine, Wade," said the inspector, "that when we've traced the full story of this boat—if we ever do—we'll find it's been through some bit!" He turned to Jessop. "Carry on. Report this, and say I've had a look at it. See that Inspector Black knows. Do you know Inspector Black?"

"Millingham," answered Jessop. "My father live at Millingham. 'Ad 'im up t'other daye fer speedin'. I know Inspector Black."

"Fine. Then now's your chance to return good for evil. Give him this message from me. Tell him I think this boat you've picked up is off a ship. Tell him to consult the files. Are you understanding me?"

"Whoy not?"

"Good. Tell him to consult the files, and to see whether he can trace any ship named the *Ferndale* that's been wrecked recently. Got that?"

"Ay."

"Repeat it."

"Whoy?"

"Because you're in for a ten-shilling note if you repeat it correctly."

Jessop's eyes grew big. He swallowed, thought, swallowed again, thought again, and said:

"Inspector Black, o' Millingham. Report this 'ere, an' see 'e gets report. See 'e knows you think she come off a ship. No. See 'e knows you bin ower the boat. *Then* see 'e knows you think she's off a ship. See 'e knows—no—tell 'im to—find out—if any ship *Ferndale*'s bin wrecked recent. And see 'e does it."

"Good enough!" laughed Kendall. "Here's your ten shillings, and now get on with it!" He stepped out of the boat and ascended to the car. "And now we'll get on with it, too, sergeant."

"Do I get ten shillings?" murmured the sergeant as the car began to move.

CHAPTER XVIII

The Trail Ends

WHILE KENDALL DROVE HE TALKED, AND WHILE HE TALKED he never took his eyes off the road ahead of him, decreasing the pace when the track he was following became faint or lost, and increasing again when the marks beckoned definitely.

"I'm still in the dark as to where we're getting, Wade," he said, "but we're certainly getting the hell of a way."

"Where was that boat found?" asked Wade.

"Three or four miles off the coast. It was empty—just as we saw it."

"And you think—?"

"I'm sure! Listen. In the hall I reconstructed a bit of yesterday for you. Now I'm going to reconstruct some more… It's queer, Wade. Sometimes you get the beginning of a story and work forwards, and sometimes you get the end and work backwards. I'm getting the middle—and I've got to work both ways! Backwards for the sense, and forward for the justice. There's a noose at the end of this, you know, for somebody. Yes, but it's another rope I'm more interested in for the moment. Damn!"

"What?"

"Hard road. The track's gone… No, there it is! Good. God bless British mud! Now, then… Seven men appear from the horizon yesterday. I don't know what time. Morning? Afternoon? Evening? Not evening. I've an idea it's the morning. Anyway, they row towards our creek—they don't sail, because the sail's not useable—they row into the river mouth, and they tie up at the landing-stage there."

"Why didn't that young feller see them?" interposed the sergeant. "Hazeldean?"

"For the very good reason that he wasn't there. He only arrived this morning."

"So he did. But he could have seen the boat."

"I'm telling you why he didn't. The boat was made fast with a rotten rope. One end you've just seen. The other is still round the post. Possibly when the last of those seven people landed there was some excitement or emotion, and the rope couldn't stand it. Anyhow, the boat got loose, and has been floating around unattended till Jessop found it."

"Wait a bit," Wade interrupted again. "Why didn't somebody else find it before Jessop, if they arrived in the morning, and it got loose then?"

"A good point. We must dispose of it. First, they *may* not have arrived in the morning. Second, if they did arrive in the morning, the boat *need* not have broken loose till the afternoon or evening. Third, there was a sea mist off this coast yesterday. The fog signal was still going this morning. I think No. 3 would dispose of your objection without Nos. 1 and 2. The boat drifted away in the mist. By the time the mist cleared and visibility became normal, it had reached the spot where Jessop found it. How does all that sound to you?"

"Pretty good," admitted the sergeant.

"And tell me if you think this is pretty good, too," went on Kendall. "That mist—it's going to help us again. If those seven people landed at the creek by accident—that is, if they were at the mercy of the mist, and simply drifted to that landing-stage, then they arrived some time after lunch, because the mist came on, roughly, at about two. Is that correct?"

"Quite," answered Wade. "Only we don't think they came by accident—do we?"

"We do not," replied Kendall. "The accident that followed would be far too much of a coincidence! And therefore, Wade, that boat arrived in the morning. Before two, anyhow. If they had been looking out for the creek mouth, they could never have found it in the mist."

"Yes, but what about this, sir?" said the sergeant. "The theory is that they died in the evening, isn't it?"

"Certainly—though always remember that a theory is something not yet proved."

"But we're working on it?"

"I think we'll find it correct."

"All right. Then if they died in the evening, and arrived in the morning—"

"Why did they waste several hours before entering oblivion? Why didn't they drop down dead on the spot, to oblige a couple of policemen?... I say, Wade, this bicycle of ours is setting a long trail! Which way now? Straight on, or over the bridge?... Over the bridge, I think. We'll try it, anyway." The car swung round to the right and crossed the water. Beyond, in a sandy lane, the cycle marks began again. "Good. Now, then. Our seven doomed people land in the morning—yesterday morning. What do they do? Go straight to the house? Not necessarily, if some big business is on. It seems to me more likely that they *would* wait till the evening. And the arrival of the mist would help to conceal them. They wait in the boat—"

"But the boat's gone!"

"I don't blame you, Wade. It's your job to trip me up. But why should the boat have drifted away just yet? Still, if it *has* gone off and left them, we'll picture them waiting, not in the boat, but on the landing-stage. And it's a picture, too, isn't it, sergeant? Seven strangers—strangers? One knew the way! Seven doomed people already half-blotted out on a misty landing-stage just inside an isolated creek mouth. Or perhaps only six."

He paused, and forced Wade's question: "Where's the seventh?"

"In the little wood. Or on the lawn. Watching the house. A shadowy figure. Or maybe there are two shadowy figures. One at the back, one at the front… and five on the landing-stage… Where am I getting? Is this sense?… And someone inside the house, watching for the shadow's, eh?… Not Miss Fenner. She's gone. She went away early… Cricket ball. Wade, that damn cricket ball. What the blazes has a cricket ball to do with it?"

"Hey!" exclaimed Wade. "Isn't it to the left here?"

The car stopped abruptly at forked roads. Kendall jumped out and looked along both forks, then went a few paces along both.

"Yes—I think you're correct," he nodded as he returned. "It isn't saying much, sergeant, but you're not quite the fool you look."

"Very kind of you to say so," grunted the sergeant.

"Not at all. Haven't you noticed how full of compliments I am?"

The car moved on again slowly.

"Wade, we don't know what happened between the arrival of that boat named *Ferndale* and the time when the seven occupants called at Haven House. Haven! My God, what a haven! We don't know what time the boat broke away. I'm not sure that it matters very much. For we know this: they entered the house—someone let them in—"

"Do we know that, sir?" interrupted the sergeant sharply.

"You mean that window at the back through which that poor miserable thief entered this morning? Wouldn't there have been a fingerprint or two—besides his—if seven others had got in through that back window? Haven't we combed the window frame, outside and in? And the ledge? Everywhere we could think of? No, they didn't enter through the back, Wade. They entered through the front. And someone let them in. And they went into the shuttered drawing-room—the shutters being nailed. They went in… If they were suspicious—if—why did they all go in so obediently?… Yes, yes, yes, but one of 'em became suspicious! Eh? The person who showed 'em in went out again into the hall—X. You remember? X. You were X. And I was the old man with the revolver. And X and the old man had a bit of a fuss at the door. And the old man fired a shot before X locked him and his companions in and got down to his devilish work through the keyhole… Whew!… And all the old man hit with his bullet was the picture of the child… Wade, put your hand very carefully into my side pocket and take out what you find. It's a faded picture—so faded that one can hardly recognise it. Still—got it? Have a try?"

"I'm blowed!" muttered the sergeant as he stared at the little piece of pasteboard. "It's—the kid!"

"That's what I thought," murmured Kendall. "It was in that boat… Hallo! Our track goes into this big flat field… Wade! Wade! Do you see anything in that clump of bushes? It *isn't* a bicycle, is it?"

CHAPTER XIX

And Another Begins

IT WAS A BICYCLE. A HERCULES. IT HAD BEEN SHOVED INTO the clump of bushes unceremoniously. A little more ceremony would have made for complete oblivion; even as it was, the machine would have been difficult to spot unless somebody had been looking for it. Kendall and Wade had been looking for it for several miles.

"I'm blowed!" said Wade.

"You shouldn't be," answered Kendall. "This is what we've come after, isn't it?"

"You don't always find what you come after," hedged Wade.

"Then your surprise is uncomplimentary to your profession, and should be kept dark. You don't always arrest a man you're after, but when you stick on the bracelets you don't say, 'Well, fancy that!' You pretend there had never been any doubt about it from the start... X didn't *ride* into those bushes, Wade."

"Are we still going on calling him X?" asked Wade.

"We might as well, in case we have to say 'I'm blowed!' when we actually discover who X is. He got off the bicycle, and then he heaved it in here. Was in a bit of a hurry, I should say."

"I'll bet he was in a hurry! Someone was after him!"

"Who?"

"Eh?"

"Who was after him—*then*?"

"Well, *you* said he was in a hurry," the sergeant pointed out.

"If you weren't smarter than your conversation, Wade," replied Kendall, "I'd heave you in the bush to join the bicycle. Fortunately, during the past few hours I've found out that you are much more useful than you sound, even if sometimes it's only by accident. But do try to avoid weak defences. Of course X was in a hurry. He was also in a flurry, which creates illusions and confuses logic. Get inside X's mind, Wade—"

"I've had enough of being X, thank you."

"I don't want you to be him this time, but to imagine him. Let's continue with his story. That'll give us a clue to his feelings, when last night *he* stood where you and I are standing now. After the little incident you and I reconstructed in the hall of Haven House—after the picture has been shot, the drawing-room door locked, and the filthy gas sent through the keyhole—X leaves the house. He rushes to the bicycle shed. He knows that seven people are dead or dying in the house he is fleeing from. Hurry? My God! Those seven ghosts are after him! He upsets his lamp in his flurry. We saw the oil marks. On the bike he jumps, along the river to the lane, along the lane to the bridge, over the bridge, and good-bye to the river, but not to the seven ghosts that are pursuing him. Out of the lane into this field… Why into this field? He has no more use for the bicycle. Why has he no more use for the bicycle?"

"P'r'aps he has no more use for himself," suggested the sergeant.

"That's one of the best remarks you have ever made," answered Kendall. "Not that I believe there's anything in it. Let's search these bushes."

But X was not in the bushes. They found no sign of him anywhere.

After five minutes Sergeant Wade made another bright remark.

"What I say is this," he observed. "If X came into this field, and if he isn't here now, he must have left it."

"So all we've got to do," replied Kendall, "is to find how he left it."

"On his feet."

"I have the size and the shape of his feet—provided X is who we think he is. Come on, Wade. We'll see whether there are any other marks along the lane."

"You mean, he might have got rid of the bicycle here, and then walked?" asked Wade, as they went back to the road.

"Yes, isn't that what *you* meant? We may be wrong in assuming the trail ends here. Where the bicycle trail ends, the boot trail may begin."

The only footprints they found were going in the wrong direction, and they did not fit Kendall's measurements.

"These may be our spoon-thief's," grunted Kendall. "Anyhow, they're not the ones I'm looking for. Hallo—what's this?"

He stooped, and picked up a small, neat little portion of brown crepe hair. One side was smooth, the other hard and messy. He examined and smelt the messy side.

"Spirit-gum," he said. "Somebody's lost a side-whisker."

"Disguise!" exclaimed Wade quickly, to get the word in first.

"Did X disguise himself?" answered Kendall.

"He might do, to get away."

"Yes… Or to receive his visitors."

"I don't get you."

"I don't think I get myself. Why should he disguise himself to receive his visitors?"

Wade scratched his head.

"P'r'haps he didn't want them to recognise him?" he suggested.

"Wade," said Kendall, "this is getting more and more devilish. We'll get back to the field."

"It's going to take some time to search all that."

"It won't be time wasted—provided I don't miss my aeroplane for Folkestone… Aeroplane. Wade! Aeroplane! You're right! This is a big field to search! A big, flat field!"

"By golly!" muttered Wade.

"Yes, we're not looking for a bicycle track this time, but an aeroplane track! X made straight for this spot. Did he expect to find the next stage of his journey waiting for him? And is *that* why—somebody—didn't cross to Boulogne *by the boat* yesterday? Eh?"

Three minutes later, they found the new marks they were searching for. Beginning a third of the way across the field, they continued towards a distant low hedge. They ended a hundred yards from the hedge.

"I don't think I need any more, for the moment," said Kendall.

In the car again, their minds were busy. Sergeant Wade expressed his thought first.

"What about that mist?" he asked.

"What about it?" replied Kendall.

"Could the aeroplane get away in the mist?"

"Pretty tricky, I should say."

"Well, then?"

"Go on."

"X didn't get away till this morning."

Kendall shook his head.

"Do you remember a remark you made to me yesterday evening?" he asked. "'Hallo—fog's letting up a bit.'"

"So it did!"

"Between seven and nine. Then it got bad again. But it may not have been so bad near the French coast. I'll find that out when I get there myself."

CHAPTER XX

Victim Number Eight

THE LIGHTS OF FRANCE GREW MORE AND MORE DISTINCT AS the *Isle of Thanet* approached Boulogne, rising and falling rhythmically on a sea of deepening grey. A harsh, deafening blast issued from the funnel, heralding the conclusion of another journey. If this had been the boat's maiden trip the loud egotistical note might have sounded appropriate, and the unfortunate folk near the funnel would have stuffed their fingers into their ears without complaint; but the trip had been made countless times, and the volume of the blast seemed to overrate the achievement.

"Well, I suppose it's necessary in a noisy age," muttered a passenger next to Kendall.

"Probably the Ichthyosaurus made a worse noise," answered Kendall.

"Pardon me," retorted the passenger, "but there is no specific evidence that Ichthyopterygia made any noise at all! On the other hand, we may presume that when the Mesozoic Allosaur attacked the Brontosaur, it snorted."

"I'm sorry," apologised Kendall. "But what I really want to know is whether a cat turns round like a dog before it sits down?"

While his fellow-traveller blinked at him, appearing to find the remark as frivolous as the inspector's red carnation buttonhole, the boat itself turned round, and backed into the harbour.

Kendall's inquiries of the passport officials, like his inquiries on the boat and at Folkestone, merely corroborated what he already knew. Dora Fenner had crossed that morning, but no other person of that surname, or answering the description of John Fenner, had been seen or heard of. Passing down the subway out of the station, he paused and looked about him. Expectation was in his eye, but the expectation soon changed to a frown.

"Not here," he murmured. "What's happened to the fellow?"

Continuing on his way, he walked slowly along. Dim shapes of ships loomed from the water on his left. He sought a particular shape, and did not find it. The trip to Boulogne was not beginning well.

At the bridge he stopped again. He lit a cigarette, and tried to make himself conspicuous. No one seemed interested in him. He grunted with annoyance, hailed a taxi, and said, "Commissariat de police." A few minutes later he was talking to the commissaire.

"I expected to be met," he said.

"Of course," answered the commissaire. "But were you not?"

"No one."

"I do not understand. As soon as we received your request I sent out my best man. I see you wear your buttonhole—he should have found you." He turned to a man at a desk. "Have you had any report from Gustav?"

"Nothing," answered the man.

"He has not been back?" The man shook his head. "No news at all?" The man shook his head again. The commissaire turned back to Kendall with a little shrug. "It is unlike him. He is reliable. Something must have happened."

"Perhaps he had to go some distance," said Kendall.

"Even so, we should have had a message. The instruction to meet you, or to report if he could not, was definite. Well, what do you suggest? We are at your disposal."

Kendall did not reply. The commissaire began to repeat his question, then stopped abruptly, and followed his visitor's gaze. It was fixed on the desk at which the other man was sitting.

"Something interests you there?" he inquired.

"May I go over and look?" asked Kendall.

"But certainly. We have our problems on this side of the water, as you have on yours—otherwise, you and I would be looking for work, eh? An aeroplane—accident." Kendall noted the little pause before the last word as he crossed the room. "Some of those items on the desk may become exhibits, to use your phrase."

"It is not a phrase we use in connection with an accident," commented Kendall.

"That is true," admitted the commissaire, rather dryly, "but this seems to have been quite an unusual accident."

Kendall stared at the exhibits. A cigarette-lighter. An unused postcard of a nude lady. A bunch of keys. A pencil. A blood-stained handkerchief...

"How—unusual?" inquired Kendall, as his roving eye paused at the next item.

"It will not waste your time to hear?" asked the commissaire, watching Kendall with interest.

"Do you and I ever waste time?" retorted Kendall.

"I waste time whenever I can, my friend," smiled the commissaire, "but so rarely I get the opportunity! The aeroplane came down some little way from here. No one saw the accident. It was not discovered at once. The aviator had been dead—how long?"

"Twelve hours or more," answered the man at the desk. A detective from the sûreté.

"He was curiously mutilated," went on the commissaire. "That made immediate identification difficult, and there was nothing on him by which to identify him. The aeroplane, also, was curiously mutilated—"

"In fact, what you're telling me," interrupted Kendall, "is that neither the man nor the aeroplane crashed, but there was a cumbrous attempt to give the tragedy that appearance?"

"Our minds move in the same grooves," nodded the commissaire. "Yes, that is our theory, without doubt."

"Have you now identified the man?"

"We have now identified the aeroplane—"

"Which will lead to the identification of the aeroplane's owner," interposed the man from the sûreté. "I expect a telephone message any moment."

"I wonder whether I can beat your telephone," said Kendall. "Was the dead man wearing a grey suit?"

"No, a brown suit."

Kendall looked surprised.

"What is that, next to the handkerchief?"

The French detective turned to the small object.

"A piece of grey cloth," he said. "It was found near the spot. Torn."

"I have torn a piece of the same cloth," replied Kendall, and produced it from his pocket.

The French detective jumped up, and the commissaire came forward.

"This bit of cloth," went on Kendall, "is from the suit of the man I am looking for—Fenner. Does it seem reasonable to you that, having torn his suit in England, the place where it was torn might be liable to a second tear—say—in France, during a struggle?" He placed the first bit beside the second bit. "I see I was wrong in thinking I could identify your dead aviator—I have no idea who he is—but I am as interested in him as you are, because I can identify his passenger."

"But—the coincidence!" murmured the commissaire.

"Forgive me, but is that remark worthy of you? When two points in the same pattern converge—"

The commissaire waved him down apologetically.

"If you are right, there is no coincidence," he admitted, "but perhaps the cloth is a coincidence? It is, after all, a very ordinary grey cloth, of a pattern much worn."

Kendall smiled, and again put his hand in his pocket.

"Your next exhibit is not so ordinary," he said. "How would you describe it?"

"False side-whisker," answered the French detective promptly.

"One. Here is the other." He drew it from his pocket. "Fenner pulled off one in England, and your dead aviator pulled off the other in France—eh? Please don't talk to me for a moment! Please don't talk to each other. If I am rude, I am rude. But in a moment I will tell you something about your aviator—though not who he is!"

He stood still, staring hard at the ground. His companions glanced at each other, with raised eyebrows, but made no attempt to break the productive silence. If their expressions said, "These strange English!" they realised that, sometimes, these strange English got somewhere.

"Listen," said Kendall, at last. "You'll soon be hearing a long story, if you're interested—and it's pretty plain now that you'll have to be—but meanwhile you know that I am investigating the deaths of seven people."

"We were impressed with the number," the commissaire assured him, "and we are abashed that we ourselves can only produce a paltry one."

"But your one increases my number to eight, and may help to discover the murderer of the lot and bring him to justice."

"You are certain it is murder, then?"

"It is risky to be certain of anything in our very uncertain profession. Even a verdict, which technically ends our uncertainty, has been known to be wrong. But for the sake of argument we can assume that this is murder, and for the sake of argument we are going to assume that—the man I am after is the murderer. Assuming so much, we have the following sequence of events to assist us. Our man leaves his house last night, after his first murders, and cycles several miles to a very large field. He hides his bicycle in a clump of bushes. Your aviator meets him. That is to say, your man in a brown suit meets my man in a grey suit. This meeting is not accidental. It has been prearranged. Perhaps hurriedly. My man is disguised. He sheds—accidentally or by design—one false side-whisker. Everything indicates hurry in that field. Your man flies my man over to France. My man drops certain damning evidence into the sea, but not his second side-whisker. He may not know that he still has it on. In due course, there is a safe landing near Boulogne, but in some isolated spot… *Was* the spot where the aeroplane was found isolated?"

The commissaire nodded.

"Then trouble brews," went on Kendall. "Or, I should say, more trouble, for enough has been left behind. What sort of trouble is this new trouble? We do not know. But we know that your man must have been thick with my man, to undertake this trip for him. We may even guess—may we?—that he was aware of my man's predicament. Either was aware when the trip started, or found out during the journey. Well—anything may happen after that, between rogues. Perhaps your man knows too much. Perhaps he threatens. Perhaps he has to be dealt with. Perhaps there is no premeditation here, but just the tragic flaring of a quarrel. Well, after seven murders, what is an eighth? Still, with an aeroplane handy, why waste the chance of a camouflage? So the eighth murder is made to appear like a landing accident at dusk... And your man is found, and mine is not. But mine has got to be found—"

The telephone broke into Kendall's words. The man from the sûreté jumped up, went to the wall, and held a brief conversation. He laid down the receiver with a grim smile.

"The dead aviator is Dr. Jones, chez Madame Paula, Haute-Ville," he said. "I suppose, Mr. Kendall, you will be coming with us?"

CHAPTER XXI

Victim Number Nine

ONLY ONE LIGHT GLIMMERED FROM MADAME PAULA'S PENSION as they approached the front door from the ramparts path. It came, very faintly, from a small window on the right of the gloomy building, making a feeble glow through a thick curtain, and the atmosphere of the place fitted the grim errand of the four men who paused in the porch. The four men were Kendall, the commissaire, the agent of the sûreté, and a gendarme.

The commissaire knocked. He knocked softly, with a somewhat ironic courtesy to the occasion, holding noise in reserve. As there was no response, he brought out a little of the noise, and knocked again more sharply.

"Do people go to bed early in Boulogne?" inquired Kendall. "Try the bell."

The commissaire did so, and also knocked a third time. Courtesy went west. The knocking and the bell echoed inside the walls of the house with an ominous insistence for anybody inside—if anybody was inside.

A little pale smudge momentarily broke the blackness of an unlit window. It came and went in a flash. Then quick, faltering steps sounded in the hall. A voice, so weak that it was hardly heard, called:

"Who is it?"

"The police," the commissaire called back. "Open the door, please, at once!"

The door opened. The men hastened in. It was Kendall who caught the figure that crumpled in the dark hall.

"A light, quick!" he said sharply.

The French detective switched on a torch, while the gendarme groped unsuccessfully for an electric switch. He found a lamp, however, and in a few moments it glowed on the strange scene. The figure in Kendall's arms was a girl, and he was staring at her intently.

"We're on the right track," he muttered. "I think I know who this girl is."

"So? Who?" exclaimed the commissaire.

"The niece of the man I'm looking for—Fenner. I've seen her portrait." The last portrait he had seen, the one he had found in the empty boat, was in his pocket. "Let's get her to a couch."

While they did so, the gendarme and the detective began a tour of exploration. The couch was against a wall, and the girl lay motionless while the two watchers regarded her with sympathetic perplexity.

"Something bad has happened here," said the commissaire.

"Follow Fenner, and you'll find something bad all along the trail," answered Kendall. "There's no rest for me till we catch that man."

"We may catch him in a moment or two."

"I doubt it, but three hounds are better than two. Do you mind if I join in the hunt?"

"I will wait here."

Kendall darted away. As he ran along a passage, someone sprang at him and seized him. It was the gendarme.

"Pardon!" grinned the man.

"Plasir," answered Kendall. "Mais, prochaine fois—comme ca!"

Returning the compliment, he seized the gendarme, imprisoning the man's arm deftly behind his back. The man's grin changed to momentary alarm, and when Kendall let him go, he regarded the released arm as though astonished that it was still there.

"Carry on," said Kendall.

The gendarme, who was really quite an intelligent fellow, sprang back to his job, while Kendall continued on his way. At the end of the passage he saw light beyond half a dozen low ascending stairs. He ran into a parlour. The room was in fair order, saving that a cushion and an open book were on the floor.

Overhead he heard hurrying footsteps. After a quick glance round, he ran out again. A few moments later he was trying a door. He had opened other doors, but this door was locked. It had the figure 2 upon it. "Yes, yes, that door!" suddenly sounded the commissaire's voice behind him. "Two! She keeps murmuring 'Two.'" As they called through the door and shook the handle, the footsteps above came hurrying down, and they were joined by the other two of their party.

"We'll have to smash this," said Kendall.

"Three shoulders should be enough," answered the commissaire, "but if you need a fourth, let me know. I'm going back to that girl."

"She's coming to?"

"Slowly. Poor child—she had been roughly handled. Someone should be by."

He vanished. His footsteps faded beyond the curtain which separated this room from the way to the hall. Three shoulders attacked the door of Numero Deux.

The lock was stubborn. Kendall seized a chair. A leg fell away as he seized it. It was not the first time the chair had been used violently that evening.

Another minute, and the work was done. The wood of the door split, and the broken panel was shoved inwards. An electric torch played through the aperture, focusing on a bed. On the bed lay a figure. There was something unmistakable in its perfect immobility. It was the figure of a dark-skinned silk merchant.

"Mon Dieu!" gasped the detective of the sûreté, while the gendarme stiffened. "Gustav!"

The ray moved from the figure on the bed to another on the floor.

"And there is the man Gustav was shadowing for me," said Kendall quietly. "Hell's been loose here. Come on—we'll get in."

CHAPTER XXII

The Conference in the Parlour

HALF AN HOUR LATER, BACK IN THE LITTLE PARLOUR OF strange memories, two roughly-handled people had recovered sufficiently to tell their stories. They had three eager listeners. The gendarme was on duty outside.

Hazeldean's story, beyond what is already known, was short. It was, in fact, mere oblivion, until the police had burst into the bedroom and helped him back to consciousness.

"After that old ruffian, Pierre, had smashed me on the head—I suppose, with the chair he was trying to reach when I last saw him—I went out like a candle," he said. His hand moved up to his bandage as he spoke. "Once or twice, I think, I nearly came to. I seemed to hear a banging—"

"You did," murmured Dora, from her armchair.

"Was that you?"

"She will tell her story in a moment," said Kendall. "It may have been us."

"Perhaps I heard both of you—it's all pretty confused," replied Hazeldean.

"Or it may have been neither. It may have been a door slamming."

"You mean, the front door?" queried the commissaire.

"Yes. Where *is* this old ruffian, Pierre?" answered Kendall. "He seems to have left in a hurry. The maid, too. You say you spoke to her, Mr. Hazeldean, just before your encounter with Pierre?"

"Yes, I asked her to stay with Miss Fenner till I returned."

"And you did not return." He turned to Dora. "Did the maid go to you? We'd like your story now."

"Yes, and told me Mr. Hazeldean had sent her," replied Dora.

"And then?"

"We waited. We were both anxious. Mr. Hazeldean was going to tell me something—something terrible that I've not heard yet"—Hazeldean caught Kendall's eye for an instant—"though I don't think anything could be more terrible than—all this. When he didn't return, Marie—that's the maid—Marie said she'd go and see what was happening. I wanted to go, but Marie insisted. It wasn't like her. I think she just wanted to help, and thought that wisest."

"I'd told her to look after you," said Hazeldean.

"Yes. And she was doing her best… But *she* didn't return, either. It was horrible! I waited till I couldn't wait any longer. Then I went after her."

She paused, and shuddered.

"Take your time, ma'moiselle," murmured the commissaire.

"Thank you—I'm all right," she answered. "Only I expect I still feel a little dizzy—and *he'll* tell you I'm not very good at telling things." She glanced at Hazeldean, and he smiled back reassuringly. "Does your head hurt?" she asked, holding on for a moment to the personal contact.

"Less and less," he replied. "What about you?"

"I'm getting better, too, though I'm still wobbly. Oh, but I must go on. Where was I?" She turned to the others. "I'm sorry I keep on breaking off. When Marie didn't come back I went after her. That's where I was, isn't it? The place was horribly quiet. It was dark, too. Someone had put out the lamp in the hall. I hadn't a match on me. I suppose I could have got one, only before I did I heard a noise.

I remember trying to call, but nothing came. I felt something like I felt when I went back to Haven House, Mr. Hazeldean—you remember, I told you about that—only this was ten times worse. I could never describe it."

"The noise came from the direction of Numero Deux?" asked Kendall.

"Yes—beyond the curtain."

"What sort of a noise?"

"Well, I'm going to tell you what it was. It was Marie, only I didn't know then—that's why it frightened me. When I went through the curtain I gave her just as big a fright. We both screamed. Then, when we got over it, I asked her what she was doing, and she said she was listening, because she felt sure she had heard something in Madame Paula's room, and the door was locked. I knew Marie had tried to get into that room, but Pierre wouldn't let her—she'd told me—and it was after Marie had failed that Mr. Hazeldean had said *he* was going in."

"Yes, and now I was in!" murmured Hazeldean, grimly.

"What did you do, Miss Fenner?" asked Kendall.

"We called, and we banged, and we knocked. No one answered us. When we gave up at last, we knew something awful had happened, though we didn't know what it was. But one by one everybody had gone. 'Shall I go for the police?' asked Marie. I'd just been going to suggest it. She said she'd go, and I let her. I'm not quite sure why I didn't go myself, or why we didn't both go. I think perhaps I didn't want to leave the house in case—well, in case Mr. Hazeldean was in it. Anyhow, that's what happened. Marie went. And as soon as she went I began banging on the door again, and—and suddenly it opened."

Her shoulders contracted as she tried to suppress another shiver.

"That must have been very unpleasant," said Kendall, quietly.

"I nearly died of fright," she admitted, with an ingenuousness that equally touched three different types of men. "You see, I didn't know what—who—was coming out. I didn't think it was Mr. Hazeldean, and somehow I didn't think it was going to be Madame Paula, though she was supposed to be resting in the room. Of course, it wasn't either. It was Pierre."

She stopped and gulped.

"Yes, of course, it would be Pierre," nodded the commissaire. "After knocking Mr. Hazeldean down, he went in to see what damage he had done, and perhaps, even, heard you or Marie coming. We can conclude, I think—and with a certain amount of excusable pleasure—that Pierre must have been quite as frightened as you, Miss Fenner."

"He was in a terrible state," she replied.

"He had heard through the door that Marie was going for the police," said Kendall. "Probably that was why he came out."

He glanced quickly at the commissaire, who shook his head. The question whether Marie had turned up at the police station was asked and answered mutely.

"What did he do?" inquired the commissaire.

"He told me to be quiet," answered Dora. "He said Madame Paula was asleep, and that it was wicked of me to risk waking her. I told him I didn't believe him. Perhaps that was silly. I'm no good at working things out when they're happening. You see, it gave him an excuse to get angrier still, or to pretend to be, and he said, 'I know you don't believe me, and that's why I can't trust you to accept what I say and to act sensibly. I'm going to lock the door again, so that Madame will not be disturbed.' He had the key in his hand. Of course, he'd taken it in with him. I tried to push past him and get into the room, and it was then that he got violent. We had a struggle, and—well, once he must have hit me quite hard. I didn't remember anything more for a bit."

"And, when you came to, I expect he'd left?" queried the commissaire.

"He must have."

"One moment, please."

The commissaire left the room quietly. Kendall guessed where he had gone. When he returned—no word was spoken during his short absence—the gendarme was no longer outside the front door. He was speeding towards the nearest telephone. The search for the absent Pierre and Marie had begun.

"Forgive me—I had to give an instruction," was all he said. "Yes, Miss Fenner? You have just come to, and Pierre has left. Yes?"

"But there isn't much more," she answered. "You see, *you* arrived soon after that, and I don't really think I came to properly at all that first time. I mean, though I managed to get up, and to know somehow that I was alone, I was still dazed, and I was still dazed when you knocked. I wasn't sure whether the knocking was real or imagination, or my heart. If it was real, I thought it might be Pierre come back again."

"Would Pierre have knocked?"

"No, of course he wouldn't. That shows the state I was in."

"And, also, it shows why you didn't answer the door at once?"

"Yes. But when I managed to get to a window and look out—I don't know how I did it—I saw several people, and I suddenly guessed that you must be the police. You see, Marie had gone for you." She stopped suddenly, and a startled look came into her eyes. "Marie! Where is Marie? She ought to be here?"

"We shall find her," answered the commissaire, quietly, "but Marie did not come to the police station."

While Dora stared, Hazeldean interposed:

"And, I suppose, Mr. Fenner did not pay you a second visit, either?"

"A—second visit?" murmured the commissaire.

"With Madame Paula, to identify the body of her husband."

The other men exchanged glances.

"Mr. Fenner has yet to pay me his *first* visit," the commissaire remarked, significantly.

"What!"

"We have not seen Mr. Fenner."

"Then how on earth," exclaimed Hazeldean, "did he know that Dr. Jones—?"

He paused abruptly.

"Your thought is our own thought," said Kendall. "Mr. Fenner did not receive his information of Dr. Jones officially, so he must have had it through some other means."

On the point of continuing, he suddenly glanced at Dora, and changed his mind. She saw the glance, however, and interpreted it with nervous intelligence.

"Please—don't stop saying anything in front of me," she exclaimed. "It isn't necessary. If it will help you to know it, I—I—"

"Miss Fenner has no reason to love her uncle," interposed Hazeldean bluntly, to help her out as she floundered, "and I'm sure she's right in thinking that this isn't a time to hide facts—although the biggest fact—by a most extraordinary sequence of circumstances and interruptions—has not yet been told her. I'll tell her that myself a little later, if I may. Meanwhile, can we concentrate on Fenner, Madame Paula, Pierre, and Marie? I saw Fenner myself. He brought the news of Dr. Jones's death—"

"Unwisely, in the circumstances," interrupted Kendall, dryly.

"No one will dispute that," answered Hazeldean, "but from what I saw of him, and from what we may guess of him, he wasn't exactly in a mood for wisdom. His one idea—we may also guess—was to get out of the house, and to take Madame Paula with him, and he used his blunder as an excuse. Does that seem reasonable?"

"Perfectly," nodded Kendall.

"Yes, and all this explains another of Fenner's omissions," Hazeldean went on. "When he left, I promised to stay here and look after Miss Fenner—and damn badly I did it—"

"You couldn't help what happened!" she interposed, quickly.

"Thank you. Perhaps not. But I'm not particularly proud… Yes, I saw you smile, Kendall, but you remember, early on, I warned you I might be a nuisance! Still, this isn't a post mortem—in that sense."

"What was the other omission?" inquired Kendall.

"Fenner was to have given a message to my crew," replied Hazeldean. "They were to have brought me some things. They haven't turned up."

"And are not likely to," commented the commissaire, as the door opened, and a tall, grave man entered the room. "Ah, doctor, you have completed your examination?" he asked, turning.

It was the doctor who had been summoned to the conference, and who had spent most of his time in Numero Deux.

"The immediate cause of your man's death is undeniably a knife," answered the doctor. "The knife, presumably, that you found under the bed. But the knife does not explain the bruise."

"May I try and explain that?" said Kendall.

"You have a theory?" asked the commissaire.

"Yes, quite a simple one," replied Kendall, "but before I give it to you I will make a little more sure of it." He turned to Hazeldean. "You know now, of course, that this silk merchant was a man from the sûreté? A man I had asked for—by telephone—to watch your movements."

"Yes, I've gathered that," answered Hazeldean. "After all, you didn't trust me?"

"You told me most definitely that you were working on your own," returned Kendall. "You were not working for the police, or even for an editor. So—I worked on my own, and hoped to tap any information you might get and not pass on to me. I hoped you would go to Boulogne, that you would find Miss Fenner's address, and that Gustav—our silk merchant—would meet me with the address and save me a lot of trouble… It is not your fault," he went on, gravely, "that poor Gustav was unfortunate. But—well—this increases one's determination to see this matter through." A shadow passed over his face. "Miss Fenner—I wonder whether—"

"I'll go? No!" The words came with unexpected sharpness. "I—I know I'm not much use—but I want to see this matter through, too. What Mr. Hazeldean said was true—I think now that it's more true than I ever thought before. About my feelings for my uncle. I—haven't any."

Kendall regarded her thoughtfully. The commissaire said:

"You, of not much use? I cannot agree to that. Permit me, Miss Fenner, to hold a high opinion of your courage. All the same, I agree it might be advisable—"

"If she stayed," Kendall changed the ending for him. "In view of that courage, I may have to ask her some more questions."

The commissaire yielded with a little sympathetic shrug.

"Meanwhile, we are still waiting for your theory," he said. "Which, remember, prints on the knife-handle may confirm or refute."

"Oh, I've not forgotten that," answered Kendall. "Can any one here tell me whether Gustav actually called at this house?"

"He did," replied Hazeldean. He related the incident.

"I see," said Kendall. "He traced you here, called, and was turned away. And that was the last you saw or heard of him alive?"

"No, I saw him from an attic window a little later," Hazeldean told him, "still waiting."

"And I saw him *at* a window—that one," added Dora.

"When? When? This is important!" The words were rapped out sharply. "Before or after Mr. Fenner and Madame Paula left?"

Hazeldean and Dora looked at each other inquiringly, and both shook their heads.

"I'm afraid we can't help you definitely there," said Hazeldean, "but my own impression, when thinking back through all the confusion, is that it was before they left. Perhaps just before. That fits your theory, doesn't it?"

"I am not allowed to choose times to fit my theories," responded Kendall. "Still, it does fit my theory. Let us follow Gustav's movements after he has traced you to the Pension Paula. He waits. He calls. He is turned away. Still, he waits—"

"And watches Mr. Fenner come along," interposed Hazeldean. "I saw that from the window. Or, strictly speaking, from the attic roof."

"Let us begin again," said Kendall. "Gustav tracks you here. He waits. He calls. He is turned away. He still waits. He watches Mr. Fenner arrive. Does Fenner see Gustav?"

"He makes no sign of it, but I think he does," answered Hazeldean.

"But there is no actual meeting?"

"No."

"Fenner enters. Gustav still waits. He tries his luck at the window. He sees Miss Fenner. He has her description. He is satisfied. He prepares to go. Remember, he was to have met me on my arrival.

Why did he not? Because he met Fenner instead. Outside this house. Fenner, also, was going. With Madame Paula. Fenner is worried. He is, as we now know, in flight. This silk merchant! He was here when Fenner arrived. He is still here! But hurrying away. Clearly, this is unpleasant! Especially to a man in Fenner's condition—a man who has blundered, and who probably knows it. So he blunders again. He tries, in some way, to interfere with Gustav. Or—yes—perhaps he frankly flies. And Pierre, who knows of and shares his master's crookedness, comes out and catches Gustav."

"If Fenner flies, why does not Gustav fly after him?" asked the doctor.

"Because Pierre prevents him," retorted Kendall. "Only that. It is obvious that Gustav cannot have been damaged far from this house—he would hardly have been carried back. No, whatever the details, Gustav was knocked out at this door. If Pierre has the strength to knock Mr. Hazeldean out, we may assume he has the strength to knock Gustav out. Gustav falls. His head hits stone. Eh?" The doctor nodded. "He is temporarily unconscious. But he will come to... And then Pierre loses his head. No one is about. He carries the unconscious Gustav inside, and locks him in Madame Paula's room, which will later serve to cover both Madame Paula's absence and Gustav's presence—"

"Yes, we were told Madame Paula was in her room," exclaimed Dora.

"Exactly. While Pierre was preparing for his own flight... But Gustav began to recover on the bed. So Pierre—finished him there. There is no blood anywhere else in the room. Or, for that matter, in the house. I think—and hope—that criminal old man had some very nasty moments when the movements of others kept him locked in Numero Deux with his own victims!... Well? What do you say?

Can we accept the pattern, while reserving judgment on some of its details?"

No one spoke for a few seconds. Dora was staring hard at the carpet, and Hazeldean moved a little closer, and patted her hand. She looked up quickly, and suddenly took his. Then the commissaire said:

"I think we can accept the pattern. One detail, as I have mentioned, will be settled by fingerprints. Unless, of course, the person who used the knife had forethought. So now we have to search for four people, two of whom may be wanted for criminal offences, one—Madame Paula—for complicity, and the other—Marie—for her safety. The hunt is on, gentlemen, and we have wasted no time—but we must see that we do not." He rose and looked at Hazeldean and Dora with a fatherliness almost embarrassing. "The invalids will be staying here, of course—with a gendarme outside to see there is no more damage."

"I'd die if I stayed here!" exclaimed Dora.

"Would you die, if you stayed on my yacht?" suggested Hazeldean. "With an old man and a small boy as chaperones?"

He never forgot the expression that leapt into her eyes at that moment, and his sympathetic imagination realised the truth behind it. She was the little child again, a child caught in a maze of nightmares; and suddenly a miracle had occurred, showing her the way out. But she could hardly believe the miracle, despite the logic that resided in the centre of it.

"Do you—mean that?" she asked, breathless.

"Of course," he answered. "Quite apart from the facts that you can't stay here, and that there seems nowhere else at the moment for you to go, I'd love it more than anything else in the world. I promised to show you the boat, you know. Well, here's the chance! You'll find she's designed for comfort as well as speed."

Kendall broke in.

"And it'll save *us* the deuce of a lot of worry," he said, and went on with a dry little smile, "You're the one point in this affair, Miss Fenner, that I can trust Mr. Hazeldean completely to look after."

"Is that a compliment?" murmured Hazeldean.

"To Miss Fenner," answered Kendall.

Hazeldean grinned.

"I'll pack my bag—it won't take a minute," cried Dora, and ran to the door, which the commissaire with his insistent politeness had opened for her. Before vanishing she paused to add, "Please—after I've left this place—never let any one bring me back here—never, never!"

CHAPTER XXIII

Beyond the Mist

LATE IN THE EVENING OF THE MOST UNNERVING DAY DORA Fenner had ever spent, she found herself walking along the ramparts between two men who gave her a strange, unnatural sense of security. She had walked along the ramparts once before that day, but then the Pension Paula had been ahead of her, waiting like an evil influence to draw her in. Now it was behind her, blotted out by a whispering darkness. Every step she took increased the distance that separated her from that hateful place, and augmented the number of intervening elms; and every step reduced the distance to a little peaceful sanctuary of whose existence she had only known for a few short hours—the quiet cabin of a yacht, perhaps swaying gently when velvet water was ruffled by a night breeze. There would be no disturbing or frightening personalities around. Only friendliness, expressed by a young man whose interest she was accepting without understanding, and by "an old man and a small boy" who, besides adding their own warm note, would soothe any frowns of Mrs. Grundy. What lay beyond the sanctuary was hidden by an impenetrable mist which she made no attempt to pierce. She was too tired.

But all at once Hazeldean pierced the mist himself.

"Worrying?" he asked, in a low voice.

"Not more than I can help," she answered.

"That means you're worrying," he replied. "Well, of course you are! But don't forget all the things I've told you."

"What things?"

She knew, but she wanted him to repeat them.

"About my sticking to you," he said. "Shall I tell you how long I mean to stick to you?" He waited a moment, while Kendall increased his pace and drew ahead. "Until I see you looking as happy as you look in that painting by your father."

"I'm afraid that will be a long time."

"I hope not. But the longer it is, the longer I'll stick. In fact, I shall probably go on sticking to you until you dismiss me."

"Oh!"

"So don't forget it. What you want is something to hang on to—something that will prevent you from feeling as though you're drifting about like a rudderless ship. Well, you're hanging on to *me*!"

"I—I seem to be."

"Unless, of course, you can give me the address of anybody else to hang on to?"

"No, I can't!"

"Hooray! Even if that's selfish. By the way, Miss Fenner, policemen aren't really so bad, are they? I think that commissaire is a most charming gentleman. I even liked the gendarme, with his snub nose. Did you notice his nose?"

"Had he one?"

"We've all got noses."

"Don't make me laugh, or I'll cry!"

"That wouldn't hurt you, though perhaps you'd better wait till we get to the *Spray*. Yes, he had a snub nose. But the chap I like best is old Kendall. Kendall of Ours. Look how considerately he's accelerated. If he accelerates much more, we'll lose him, and we mustn't do that, because there's a car waiting for us at the bottom of the next steps. Shrewd fellow, Kendall—knows when he's wanted, and knows when he's not. Hullo—what's up?"

"Nothing," said Dora, "but I just feel a bit weak."

"All empty like?"

"Yes."

"And head going round and round like?"

"Yes."

"And knees a bit wobbly like?"

"Yes."

"Then we're a pair, because I feel all empty like, and my head's going round like, though my knees aren't quite wobbly like. Isn't all this lucky? It gives us a logical excuse for holding each other up."

He put his arm round her.

"Now I *am* crying," she said, as he drew her closer beside him.

"And I told you to wait!" he reprimanded her. "All right, have it your own way, only do it softly, or Kendall will hear. Ah, here are those steps!"

They turned into the little opening that twisted down to the bottom of the wall. They emerged at La Porte des Dunes, and saw through the archway the smudge of a waiting car. Behind them brooded the Haute-Ville, seeming drowsily to watch them go. It contained its joys, but to them it was just a bad dream, saving that it contained the spot where they had met.

Kendall watched them enter the car with a smile. Their world was not his, but he understood it, and though he had not heard a word of their conversation, he could have written a fairly accurate report of its tenor.

"Where?" he asked Hazeldean. "You know where you left your boat."

"Quartier Saint-Pierre," answered Hazeldean, and named the exact spot.

The car ran down the wide hill, then turned into the narrow shopping streets that led in the direction of the quay. Soon the quay itself came into view, with dark shapes and little lights upon it. "Here we are!" called Hazeldean. The car slowed down and stopped. A moment later he exclaimed, "Wait a minute! Is this right?… I'm not sure…"

He jumped out. Two figures loomed at him. A large one and a small one. His eye brightened at their familiar shapes.

"Hallo, Bob!" he cried. "Where've you moved her to? I thought I'd mistaken the spot."

He glanced at the vacant water-space where, earlier, the *Spray* had been.

"I ain't moved 'er," answered Bob.

"What do you mean?"

"I thought, mebbe, *you* 'ad, sir, while we was lookin' for you at Wimereux."

"Looking for me—at Wimereux?"

As he repeated the astonishing words, Kendall joined him gravely.

"So that's how they did it!" he murmured. "Well, we don't need much more to complete the evidence!"

"Bob! Who told you to look for me at Wimereux?" demanded Hazeldean, sharply.

"Grey-'aired gent, it was, sir," replied Bob.

"Yes! Go on!"

"'E come along—"

"Alone?"

"I see a lidy with 'im, sir," interposed the boy, eagerly, "before they got 'ere, that was, but when they got 'ere, she'd bin lef' be'ind."

"I never seed no lidy," muttered Bob, unhappily.

"No, gran'fer didn't, but I did," insisted Joe, "but when I look again, she's be'ind something."

"Well—carry on, Bob," said Hazeldean, "and look sharp!"

"'E come along," repeated Bob, "and 'e sez,'Is that the *Spray*?' and I sez, 'Ay, ay,' and 'e sez, 'Owner's name 'Azeldean?' and I sez, 'Ay, ay,' and then 'e sez, 'Well, 'e's got some bizziness at Wimereux, that's my 'otel,' 'e sez, 'and 'e's got to stay the night, and 'e wants you there too, and to take along a bag of 'is things.' 'Wot's the 'otel?' I sez. ''Otel Ongleterre,' 'e sez, 'a tram will get you there in twenty minutes, and 'e wants you at once, 'cos one of you may 'ave to bring a message back to someone at the Casino before 'e goes.'" Bob paused rather guiltily, and gulped. "So we went, sir. And—and there wasn't no 'Otel Ongleterre, the on'y Ongle was Ongles and Bans, but you weren't there, so arter waitin' awhile, sir, we came back with our bags"—the bags were on the ground beside him—"and the boat was gone."

Hazeldean glanced at Dora, who had now joined them from the car and who was listening in astonishment to this new development.

"If you're thinking about me, you mustn't!" she exclaimed, quickly.

"I am thinking about you, and I must!" he answered.

"Yes, everything shall be thought of," said Kendall, "and I can take you to a good hotel that will cover the immediate situation. But, do you know what *I'm* thinking of?"

"What?"

"The luck of some people who don't deserve it. Look!"

He pointed to the water. White shapes were creeping along the surface, wiping more solid substance out.

"The mist," said Kendall. "It's back again."

CHAPTER XXIV

Half-Way House

THERE WAS NO MIST ON THE WATER WHEN, SOME WEEKS LATER, Detective-Inspector Kendall stepped on board a trim yacht named *Spray II*, moored at a river mouth somewhere in Africa, to renew his acquaintance with two young people. Hazeldean gripped his hand firmly, and Dora—a very different Dora from the timid girl he had first met in the shadow of the ramparts—was equally happy to see him.

"My advice has proved good, Miss Fenner," exclaimed Kendall. "I hardly recognise you!"

"*All* the change isn't due to you, Mr. Kendall," she answered, with a glance at Hazeldean.

"But Kendall started the ball rolling by clearing us out of a bad atmosphere into a good one," said Hazeldean. "That was the smartest bit of work he ever did!"

"I agree," nodded Kendall, "though some of the credit must also go to the commissaire and the doctor. It was the doctor, in fact, who warned me that Miss Fenner might go under if she didn't escape at once from policemen and publicity."

"It—it was that last news—about what had happened at Haven House—that nearly finished me," murmured Dora.

"And the policemen and the publicity would have quite finished you," nodded Kendall. "That's why I packed you both off. I didn't need you any more—just then."

"Just then?" repeated Hazeldean.

Kendall smiled.

"Those two words shouldn't surprise you. I named this date and this place for a possible reunion—and here I am."

"Well, here *we* are," responded Hazeldean. "Having obeyed you in all things. Not only have we cut ourselves adrift from everything but winds, tides, fishes, birds and mosquitoes, but we've kept this date for you. Do you know we've been hanging around here for a fortnight? I only hope you're going to make it worth our while! There's a particular mosquito we've named George, who calls regularly every night to sing to my nose, that I'm just longing to get away from."

"We'll get away from him," promised Kendall. "Do you still stock that excellent sherry I once tasted in a smaller river mouth in Essex?"

"Thus tactfully," smiled Hazeldean, "a smart detective steered the conversation towards the true object of his visit."

"Which was not the sherry," said Kendall.

When they were seated in the saloon, with the sherry before them, Kendall suddenly asked, "How much more do you two know than when you sailed off?"

"Very little," replied Hazeldean. "You can take it—nothing. We did the thing thoroughly. Dropped right out when you let us go, and haven't worried about papers. We don't even know—whether you've found any one yet?"

"Not Mr. Fenner," answered Kendall. "Yet."

"No trace of him since he took my boat and vanished into the mist?"

"None."

"What about the others?"

"We found Marie the day after you left."

"Where?"

"At the pension."

"At the pension? She went back?" exclaimed Dora.

"Pierre chased her back," replied Kendall. "He caught her up before she left the ramparts and turned her round again. I don't know just how he managed it. Marie doesn't know herself. He scared the life out of her, and when we found her she was nearly out of her mind."

"But I don't understand!" exclaimed Hazeldean. "Marie wasn't at the pension when you came along."

"As a matter of fact, she was," answered Kendall. "We only unearthed her just in time. Mr. Fenner had a secret workshop at both ends—Boulogne and Benwick—and Master Pierre knew all about it."

"You mean, he'd hidden her there?"

"Practically buried her there. But, as I say, we got her out of the cellar in the nick, and she's been looked after."

"Poor Marie!" murmured Dora.

"Not so poor as she was," corrected Kendall, with a dry glance at Hazeldean. "She's writing her life story."

Hazeldean laughed.

"Or, do you mean, somebody else is?" he asked.

"Well, I expect somebody else shares the cheques with her. Perhaps, after all, you should have stayed behind, Hazeldean, to pick up the journalistic crumbs?"

"I doubt whether this particular crumb would have been in my line."

"And it must really be a very tiny crumb," added Dora. "Marie's life, I should think, must have been very uneventful."

"Uneventful?" retorted Kendall. "She was the youngest of thirteen children, always wanted to go on the stage, has fallen out of three windows, been in twenty-eight fires, and once walked home under Maurice Chevalier's umbrella. By the time we get back she will probably be engaged to a film star!… Well, let us leave Marie to the romancers. Personally, I found Pierre and his truth far more interesting."

"Oh! You found Pierre?" exclaimed Hazeldean.

"Yes, we found Pierre," responded Kendall. "After Marie. He led us a dance, though, and was as slippery as an eel. He beat us twice. The third time we got him in a Paris attic. We had to get him, and we had to make him talk. Oh, yes, Pierre's talk was far more interesting than Marie's writings. He worked for Dr. Jones, just as Dr. Jones worked—sometimes—for Mr. Fenner. And Pierre had a habit of hearing a lot more than he was ever told."

"I learned of the connection between Jones and Mr. Fenner from Pierre. I learned how they met, and how they worked together, and also where Madame Paula came in. I'm afraid—it's not particularly—"

"Never mind what it is, please go on," interposed Dora. "One thing I expect you learned from Pierre was that Dr. Jones was trying to make love to me."

"Yes, I learned that," nodded Kendall.

"And my uncle wanted it, so that he could make love to Madame Paula. Did Pierre tell you that?"

"Pierre knew that. He also knew what was in a letter Dr. Jones wrote Mr. Fenner the day before your last visit to Boulogne—"

"Yes, one came in the morning!" exclaimed Dora.

"Do *you* know what was in it, Miss Fenner?"

"No."

"I needn't mince matters?"

"I've told you."

"Well, it was this letter that gave your uncle his first desire to go to Boulogne that week-end. Dr. Jones was impatient. You were giving him no encouragement. Unless your uncle brought you over and altered your mood, the collaboration was at an end, and Dr. Jones would reveal something he knew."

Dora was silent for a moment. Then she said quietly, "No, I didn't know that, though it doesn't surprise me. What was it Dr. Jones threatened to reveal?"

"I don't know. Nor does Pierre. If Pierre had known, you can be sure the commissaire would have got it out of him—you have only seen that polite gentleman on his best behaviour, I assure you!"

"Then what was the nature of the collaboration?" asked Hazeldean.

"To explain that, I'll first explain how it arose," answered Kendall. "I've traced a good deal about both Mr. Fenner and Dr. Jones, and everything fits perfectly. When your father was dying, Miss Fenner, he wrote to his brother in South Africa, your uncle, in the hope of patching up an old quarrel. John Fenner would inherit the house—Haven House—and as you were still a child, your father hoped your uncle would take his place, look after you, and make a home for you."

"Yes, I know that," said Dora. "He told me before he died. He died before Uncle John came."

"Did you also know that your uncle sailed from South Africa in the *Good Friday*, but arrived at Southampton on the *William George*?"

"Yes. At least, I knew the first ship had been wrecked, and that Uncle John was the only person saved."

"He was picked up by the *William George*. No trace was ever found of the *Good Friday*. Your uncle said there had been a mutiny, and that everything, including the wireless, had been smashed before the ship went down. He was in a pretty bad condition when he was rescued. Practically unconscious, and clinging to the last portion of the small boat he'd got away in. The doctor of the *William George* looked after him, and kept him in his cabin. The doctor was Dr. Jones.

"I've traced the record of the *William George*'s surgeon at that time. It isn't much of a record. His conduct had not been professional, and he'd been struck off the Medical Register.

"But now, apparently, that didn't matter. The shipwrecked man—John Fenner—whom he'd brought back to life remained his friend. Dr. Jones had a lady friend, also, in Boulogne, who needed money to keep her pension going. Your uncle supplied that money, Miss Fenner, and enabled Dr. Jones to marry the lady and become her permanent boarder."

"Wasn't Mr. Fenner rather elaborate in his gratitude?" suggested Hazeldean.

"Extremely elaborate," answered Kendall. "Especially as he needed his inheritance to assist him with his invention. All his money went to the invention and to Dr. Jones. That explains why he pleaded poverty to his niece—"

"And why you had to do all the housework, Dora," said Hazeldean. "Of course, what Dr. Jones got out of it wasn't due to gratitude, but to blackmail."

"Yes, obviously," replied Kendall. "Dr. Jones learned something while he was bringing John Fenner back to life in his cabin on the *William George*—and what he learned will prove, when we learn it ourselves—to be the kernel of the mystery."

"How are we going to learn it?"

"There are two possible sources. One is from John Fenner himself—the other I'll tell you shortly. Jones, after settling down with Madame Paula in the pension, seems to have led a useless sort of a life there. His inglorious career had also included a short term in the Air Force, and he took up flying again as a hobby. He flew Fenner across to Boulogne more than once. I found a cable in a drawer of Jones's bedroom. It said: 'Agree. William George. Usual. Wait.' Guessing that the words 'William George' were used by them for the aeroplane—probably covering some recognised arrangement—we can elaborate this message into something along the following lines: 'Agree to the terms of your letter this morning. Fetch me by aeroplane. Will meet you in the usual place. Wait till I turn up.' The usual place, of course, was the isolated field where Wade and I found Fenner's bicycle." He paused as his mind travelled back. "That mist, you know—it might have played the devil with all their arrangements, and instead it was on their side right the way through. It lifted when they needed to see, and came on again when they needed not to be seen."

"We're piercing plenty of mist now, anyway," commented Hazeldean.

"Before we've finished we'll pierce the lot," answered Kendall. His eyes rested for a moment on the little round of brilliant blue water that danced and sparkled through the porthole, as though he were dwelling on the contrast. Then he went on: "Matters came to a head on that last trip across the water. I dare say the two men quarrelled *en route*, but Fenner had to get over. When they landed, however, and Jones got nasty—we can be sure they had plenty to quarrel about—he had to be dealt with. Well, we know what happened to Jones."

"May I interrupt for a moment?" asked Hazeldean.

"Of course. Have you found a flaw?"

"No, but Madame Paula said that Mr. Fenner had arrived on the evening before—"

"Yes, by the boat I missed," added Dora.

"Madame Paula was lying," answered Kendall, "which proves the extent to which she was interested in Mr. Fenner. She was ready to lie for him and fly with him. Whether he told her everything, we don't know; but a woman like that generally knows on which side her bread is buttered, and by now she probably had little feeling left for her husband."

"She hated him," said Dora.

"She had every reason to," replied Kendall. "And so, Miss Fenner, had you. We won't waste any special sympathy over Dr. Jones. But—the seven victims whose deaths preceded that of Dr. Jones? I think we shall find a very different story here."

He stared at his half-empty glass, made a movement to finish it, then pushed it away.

"Those seven people were finished off most devilishly by a new form of gas which is interesting our authorities at this moment," he continued. "Probably Fenner hoped to make his fortune out of that gas. Probably Jones did also. Well, the gas was convenient for another purpose not originally thought of—and now we come to the cricket ball."

"There's one question I'd like to put first," interposed Hazeldean. "Where does Pierre come into all this? Is he just a naturally bad character who happened to be handy, or does he fit into the jig-saw?"

"He fits into the jig-saw," replied Kendall. "He was a steward on the *William George*. Jones took him along with him to Boulogne. Exactly why, I can't say. We're satisfied we've got all the truth we can out of him—which is quite enough to go on with as far as Pierre himself is concerned—and that he doesn't know the nature of the original secret between Jones and Fenner. But I expect he smelt a rat—maybe as far back as on the boat—and that Jones thought it wise to have him under his wing."

"He recognised a brother of the breed!" added Hazeldean. "Well—what have you found out about the cricket ball?"

"Very little, for certain. Rather less, by presumption. But the complete story—well, we're on the way to that now, I hope."

"We?"

"You, I, Miss Fenner, and your crew."

The atmosphere in the cabin suddenly tightened. Kendall himself seemed to feel it, for he added quickly: "Of course, we needn't include Miss Fenner."

"Mr. Kendall," answered Dora, "do you seriously think you can leave me out?"

Kendall knew that he couldn't.

"Right! Very well, that's settled. Now, what we know for certain about the cricket ball is that it came through a window and gave Mr. Fenner a severe shock. That it increased his desire to leave Haven House, supplying a second urgent motive for going to Boulogne. And that it was an old ball. Expert opinion suggests from five to ten years as the age. I verified the fact that balls of this make and type were obtainable from five to ten years ago in Cape Town—from where John Fenner sailed. Although the ball has known an extraordinary amount of wear and sea-water, the impressions of two small letters are just decipherable. They've helped. By the way, Miss Fenner, your father—John Fenner's brother—also came from South Africa, didn't he?"

"Yes, he was born there, and he had meant to go back when he left," replied Dora, "but he met my mother in England and stayed to marry her."

"And he never went back at all?"

"No. I think Uncle John was rather upset. There were only the two of them, and they were in business together."

"Did your Uncle John ever speak about this?"

"To me? Only once, that I can remember. It was just after he arrived at Haven House. 'Your father deserted me,' he said, 'but, you see, I'm not deserting him, and bear him no ill-will.'"

"I don't see why he should," commented Kendall dryly, "since he was coming into the property! You've got the words pretty pat."

"Yes. They were among his first words, and I think one would remember those. Besides—they seemed so—stilted."

Kendall nodded. "And your mother?"

"She died a year after I was born."

"I see. Yes… Well, to return to the cricket ball, I've told you all I know; and now here are some presumptions. Your uncle had seen that cricket ball before, and he interpreted it correctly as a warning. He sent you off, in consequence, to Boulogne. Then, in the evening, he received seven visitors, disguised as his own butler. Then he went to fetch himself, but fetched something else instead—his gas—which he sent through the keyhole… I've identified some of those seven visitors."

"You have?" cried Hazeldean.

"Yes. From the list of passengers and crew who were on the *Good Friday*, the ship he sailed on, from some descriptions, and from a group photograph. Fenner lied when he said he was the only one saved. The photograph, taken just before the ship sailed, shows the third officer, Harold Brown. He is one of the seven. It also shows a rather mannish-looking woman walking along a gangway. If it had been taken a couple of seconds later, we should have lost her, for she's only just on the picture. Look."

Now he drew the photograph from his pocket and laid it on the narrow cabin table. Hazeldean and Dora peered over it, and Hazeldean gave an exclamation.

"You recognise her?" asked Kendall quietly.

"In—the chair," murmured Hazeldean.

"That was my impression. In spite of the usual theory, photos sometimes lie, but these features seem too distinctive to mistake. I haven't got her name—just the picture. Do you recognise any more?"

Hazeldean studied the photograph.

"One more, I think," he said at last. "The fellow on the couch?"

"Arthur Lawson," nodded Kendall. "And looking—if I may say so—more vapid in life than he looked in death. That the lot?"

"No!"

It was Dora's voice this time. She was peering over Hazeldean's shoulder. She touched a small figure leaning idly over a rail, without betraying any interest in the photographer.

"Well?"

"Uncle John!"

"Yes, there's not much doubt about it. That proves that the whole of his story was not fiction—he was on that ship—and, in addition, we find three of the seven victims accounted for. I'm particularly disappointed not to find the old gentleman who fired the shot, but though he's not in the picture, I am concluding he was on the ship. I am also concluding that the two seamen were on the ship. That brings the number up to six. And the seventh I have identified by a description. This, Hazeldean, is the tall brown-haired man who was lying nearest the door. The man with the scar on the back of his head. I found out something rather interesting about him—including how he got that scar. He was cricket mad. Played regularly for his club in Port Elizabeth—William Miles, I've looked up some of his scores—and he kept up his enthusiasm even after receiving a crack on the head through looking the wrong way. As a matter of fact, that crack on the head seems to have made him madder about the game than ever, because afterwards he carried the ball about with him wherever he went—as a mascot! Queer that, eh? And mighty interesting… Let's have your thought, Hazeldean. You're wondering about something?"

"I'm wondering whether William Miles had his mascot in his pocket when the *Good Friday* went down," replied Hazeldean.

"I'm not—I'm damn sure he did!" answered Kendall, with a grim smile. "But now I want to talk about another ship—the *Ferndale*. You remember, the name *Ferndale* was on the abandoned boat our seven victims arrived at the creek in."

"Have you proved that?"

"Sufficiently. You haven't forgotten that little photograph of Miss Fenner I found in it."

"Yes, but how do you explain that?" asked Dora.

"We'll find the explanation presently," returned Kendall, "and meanwhile it serves as a connecting link. It belonged, obviously, to one of those seven people. Two separate mysteries relating to your family would be too much of a coincidence! Now, then, about the *Ferndale*. We had no difficulty in tracing the origin of that little boat. Eleven months ago a cargo steamer named *Ferndale*, bound for Buenos Aires from Cape Town, met a storm and was driven off her course. The storm was a terror, and she went farther south than she had ever been. The only ultimate damage, however, was a lost boat—in addition to lost time. Yes? You're wondering about something else?"

"Pretty obvious what I'm wondering, isn't it?" responded Hazeldean. "That lost boat seems to have travelled the hell of a distance!"

"South?"

"And north!"

"Yes. But is that all you're wondering about?"

"What do you mean?"

"Doesn't it strike you that there's a surprising amount of South Atlantic about this business?"

"Well, of course. The *Good Friday* went down there, the *William George* picked Fenner up there, and now—the *Ferndale*. But if they're all part of the same story, you'd expect to find 'em in a bunch."

"Can't you add something else to the bunch?"

Hazeldean thought, then shook his head.

"Your mind's been off this case lately—mine hasn't," said Kendall. "What about a piece of paper? A piece of paper on one side of which a murderer had written in printing letters: 'With apologies from the Suicide Club,' in a cumbrous attempt to shift the blame—"

"By God—yes!" exclaimed Hazeldean. "And on the other side of the paper—"

"One of his victims managed to scribble, in his last moments of consciousness: 'Particulars at address 59·16S 4·6E. G.' Suppose 'G' was the first letter of a sentence intended to start with the word 'Go,' and suppose 59·16S and 4·6E represent latitude and longitude. By the way, did you mention this piece of paper to Fenner? I suppose you did?"

"Yes, I mentioned it," nodded Hazeldean.

"Then I've a hunch that's where *Spray I* has gone," said Kendall, "and where *Spray II* is going to follow!"

Dora had suddenly left the table. Now she returned breathlessly with a map. She spread it out before them on the flat surface.

"Just blue water," murmured Hazeldean.

"Call that a map?" retorted Kendall, and produced another.

Kendall's map was a large scale chart of a small portion of South Atlantic. Hazeldean knew the charts well, for he used them himself, though he did not possess one as far south as this.

"See that tiny dot?" said Kendall.

"By Jove!" murmured Hazeldean.

"Well," asked Kendall, "what about paying the tiny dot a surprise visit?"

CHAPTER XXV

Back to the Source

THE TINY DOT MATERIALISED FROM A MARK ON A MAP TO A point on blue water.

At first, when Hazeldean directed Dora's straining eyes towards it, she could see nothing. The horizon looked as deserted and unbroken as it had looked for many days—ever since, in fact, they had finally left the African coast and a continent had dissolved into an endless sea; but soon the dot grew into her vision, and as it expanded, gaining breadth and height while *Spray II* rode forward on a fresh north-easterly breeze, she discovered that not until now had she really and truly believed in it. That dot had been a thing to talk about, a horribly fascinating magnet for theories. It could never become solid ground over which they would one day walk towards the secret in its heart. But here was the day, and here was the solid ground—no longer theories, but realities. The dot became a bleak, grey thing, puffing itself out slowly like a jagged, evil monster.

The eyes of her male companions were alive with eager elation, but Dora herself endured some moments of secret panic. Wouldn't it have been better to let the monster sleep on, instead of permitting it to raise its head from the sea and notice them?

"You stay on board, eh, while Kendall and I investigate," came Hazeldean's voice in her ear.

She turned to him with a smile.

"What made you suggest that?" she asked.

"I don't know. I thought it might be a good idea."

"In case there's any danger?"

"Of course there'll be no danger!"

"Then why should I stay on board?" She shook her head. "Thanks, I'm going with you."

"And thus she forced the truth out of him!" said Hazeldean. "The reason I suggested it was because you looked worried—I mightn't have known if you hadn't made such a grim effort to look happy! Now, then, it's *your* turn for frankness. Am I talking through my hat?"

She laughed and answered, "No, you're not. I *was* going through some funny moments; but one doesn't pay any attention to them, so that's that!"

Before long, however, she went through another funny moment. Her eyes opened wide with astonishment. They had altered their course, and were beginning to run round the isle to find some accessible spot, and now the formidable masses of rock, often dropping sheerly into angry, noisy water, gave way to a sudden stretch of beach that appeared to be densely populated.

"Look!" she gasped.

"Yes, and I keep on looking," retorted Hazeldean. "You don't really suppose those are cousins and aunts, do you, who've come along to give us a welcome?"

The reception committee turned out to be a large group of penguins, watching their approach from the shore with vaguely indignant apathy. As the boat drew closer inshore, the indignation became less vague, and agitation set in.

"Don't disturb 'em yet," said Kendall. "I'd like to go all round before we land."

Hazeldean glanced at him, then nodded, and once more altered the course. He realised Kendall's object. It was to find out whether

Spray I had preceded them. But there was no sign of the ship, or of any life at all on the island apart from the penguin colony and the sea birds that swooped or floated above them.

"O.K.?" queried Hazeldean, when they had completed the circle.

"O.K.," replied Kendall; but his rather puzzled expression added mutely: "Let's hope so!"

A few minutes later, *Spray II* lay at anchor in the shelter of a rock-formed harbour, and the little landing boat, an Indian *cayuca*, had slid across to the strip of beach where the agitated penguins were already in retreat. By the time Kendall, Hazeldean and Dora had landed and the boat had been pulled ashore, the last of the displaced population were waddling over a ledge to join an invisible indignation meeting.

"Well, here we are!" exclaimed Hazeldean.

"And I can't say I'd choose the spot for a summer holiday."

"Nor would I," agreed Dora.

"Probably the last people who stayed here weren't choosers," observed Kendall.

"True," murmured Hazeldean. "Any sign of them?"

Kendall did not answer, but stood still, gazing about him. Hazeldean was reminded of the moment when the detective had originally arrived at Haven House, and had delayed investigation till he had registered and fixed his first impressions. The moment returned to his memory so vividly that the horrible sound made by the "buzzer" seemed to echo once more in his ears...

"Ha!"

The exclamation came swiftly and sharply, and an instant later Kendall was running towards a rock. His abrupt movement was like a continuation of the memory, under strangely different circumstances, for he had also run suddenly into Haven House to bawl to the telephone operator to stop the buzzer.

"I—I wonder what he's seen?" gulped Dora, moving a little closer to Hazeldean.

"We'll know in a second," he replied, resisting the temptation to follow. "My sight's good, but his is better!"

They watched him reach the rock, bend, and study its flattish face. Then they watched him turn and begin pacing his way back. He paced with the methodical regularity of measurement, and Hazeldean found himself counting the paces while wondering what on earth it was all about. Seventeen—eighteen—nineteen—twenty—twenty-one—twenty-two.

He stopped and beckoned to them. When they reached him he took something from his pocket with a very odd expression. It was the old cricket ball.

"Cracked William Miles stood here and bowled this ball at that rock," he said, with a solemnity that was almost reverent. "That rock has three rough wickets carved upon it."

"Whew!" murmured Hazeldean, while Dora's heart raced.

"Yes, they've all been here," said Kendall. "All seven of them. No, eight of them. Fenner, too. They've all been here. And what happened? What happened?"

Ghosts peopled the lonely beach. A sense of stifling unreality pervaded the place, providing the atmosphere of a dream under gas... gas...

"What's that over there?" said Kendall.

He was off again, and this time they followed him. They caught him up at the back of the beach as he paused under a rocky cliff and bent over a circular object. It was a broken, blackened hoop.

"This was once round a barrel," he said.

"And there's a bit of the barrel," answered Hazeldean, pointing.

Along a rough path leading inland and upwards between the rocks they found other things: a split plank, two empty rusty tins, the indecipherable cover of a book, a fragment of rock wedged in a grotesquely-shaped wooden handle. The theory that this was used as a hammer gained colour from a long bent nail lying near it. A game of "Noughts and Crosses," scratched on a large stone; some filthy, sodden material that had once been part of a sail; a broken oar.

Each object had some story; each formed a part of the hidden history of eight ghosts who flitted formlessly along the trail.

Presently the trail widened into a scarred, uneven plateau. To continue meant steeper climbing, for the plateau was half-enclosed by precipitous heights. On the beach side, however, the ground dropped, and beyond untidy slopes of tangled vegetation, through which ran a stream, were glimpses of the sea. One glimpse revealed *Spray II* looking like a toy.

"I expect this was their camp," said Kendall.

"Yes, there's more debris here," replied Hazeldean.

Dora slipped on something loose. As she looked down to see what she had stepped on, she felt a queer little tug at her heart.

"What is it?" asked Hazeldean.

She picked up the object. It was a home-made cricket bat.

"I feel like crying," she said.

"Perhaps I do, too," he answered, "only, you know, we mustn't." He turned to Kendall. "What do you make of all this? Are you developing any theory?"

"Are you?" returned Kendall.

He moved towards a mound of stones. A stake had been firmly planted in the centre, and across the top of the stake was an oblong of wood, resembling a notice-board.

"Keep off the grass?" inquired Hazeldean.

He was joking purposely, but the joke fell flat. Kendall did not respond. He was reading four other words carved deep into the wood:

FIAT JUSTICIA RUAT CÆLUM

Dora asked their meaning. Hazeldean translated soberly: "Let justice be done though the heavens should fall."

"It shall be done," promised Kendall.

Hazeldean looked at him curiously.

"You feel this pretty much, don't you?" he asked.

"It's just another case," replied the detective.

"Only it's got you?"

"Somehow." He glanced again at the cricket bat, then suddenly exclaimed, "Yes, but we weren't brought all this way just to see relics!"

"This monument is a pretty good one," commented Hazeldean. "Still, I agree there must be something else."

"Of course there's something else," answered Kendall, "and we've got to find it! What do we know so far? Eight people were washed up here—"

"Do we know that?"

"I know it, and you know it, and—"

"I know it," interposed Dora.

"Well, that's enough to go on with. The jury can wait. They were washed up here, and they played cricket. One got home first, and gave out that he was the only one. The other seven followed him—after erecting this monument. *Fiat justicia ruat cælum*. They must have felt those words pretty deeply to have cut them so deeply!

Fiat justicia ruat cælum. I suppose a few stores got washed up with them, and they had birds, fish and berries. There's some vegetation here. *Fiat*—where did they sleep? In the open? You'd look for caves, wouldn't you? Let's look for caves. I don't see any. What about round that jut? Come on!"

He started off again. They clambered over the rough ground towards a rocky projection that screened a portion of the plateau from their view. Beyond, they found what they sought: three holes in the cliff, two large, one small.

They entered a large one. It led to dark, cold space. As Kendall struck a match, and the light flickered on the walls, he remarked, "Bedroom for three." They found a few pathetic evidences of occupation.

The second large hole took them into a second cave of similar size. "Bedroom for three," repeated Kendall as he struck another match. "That's six."

The smaller hole led to a space of different shape. It was long and narrow, and the end twisted through rocky walls. "Bedroom for two," said Kendall when they reached the end. "Which two?"

They waited while the match flame moved slowly along the little length of wood. The walls blinked, as though unused to light.

"Well—just this," murmured Hazeldean, as the light began to die.

"Just what?" came Kendall's voice a second later through the darkness.

"Just a cave."

"You missed something in that last flicker."

"Did I? What?"

Kendall struck another match. The cave glowed into life again. He advanced the flame to a ledge in the wall. On the ledge was a small pencil stump.

"By Jove!" exclaimed Hazeldean.

"Recognise the breed?" asked Kendall.

"I—I'm not sure."

"Never mind. Go on."

"Red. Wasn't the pencil stump you found in the grey-haired man's hand red?"

"It was."

"But, after all, there are millions of red pencils."

"Quite correct. And—again, after all—we know that grey-haired man was here. Still, it's interesting that the end of this stump isn't smooth, so may be a portion of a longer pencil that was broken in half. I wonder whether the other half found its way to Haven House?"

"And I wonder what this half wrote," added Hazeldean.

"We're going to find what it wrote," said Kendall.

Now he moved the match flame along the wall. Its rough, uneven surface became alive with little moving black shadows as the light passed along. The shadows looked like black slits that grew fat and thin, and vanished. But one black slit did not vanish or change its size. Kendall inserted two fingers in it, and drew out a thin note-book. The match went out. Hazeldean felt something leaning against him.

"I think I'm suffocating!" gasped Dora. "Please—I must get out."

They turned and left the cave. In the free air, she sat upon a rock, recovering from a fit of trembling.

"I'm sorry—but that grey-haired man," she murmured, "he seemed to be there."

Kendall looked up from the book he had opened.

"He was there," he said. "And now he's going to talk to us."

CHAPTER XXVI

The Voice of a Diary

WELL, WE ARE OFF AT LAST. ALL THE FUSS AND THE BUSTLE are over, the passengers have been sorted from the non-passengers who came to see them off—nobody came to see *me* off!—and the funnel has made its horrible noise. The photographer nearly missed getting ashore. Serve him right if he had, for he and his damned camera were a curse. I did my best to dodge him. But he just scuttled down the gangway before it was withdrawn, and now the water is widening between me and South Africa, and I am wondering whether I shall ever see it again. Probably not. That's a queer thought. I wonder whether people ought to leave the land they were born in? It was a woman who caused poor Henry to stay away, and now it is another woman—though of course a small one this time—who is carrying me away from my own roots. Perhaps I wouldn't have done it if he hadn't tempted me with that little photograph. Dora must be a jolly little kid. Yes, if we can get used to each other, we may make a team! But, of course, I have another reason—

Hallo, that was a roll! I hope the *Good Friday* is going to prove good! The first word of the name is all right, but the second might worry superstitious people—especially as to-day is Friday. Fortunately, I am not superstitious. At least, I don't think I am.

Well, what about a drink?

*

Met a queer fellow while having that drink. I thought he was dotty at first, and am not sure that he isn't! Came to my table with his glass, sat down and asked whether I thought Bradman was a greater cricketer than W. G. Grace. Told him I didn't know and didn't care. This both astounded him and depressed him. He took a cricket ball from his pocket and began shooting it from his hand to the crook of his elbow, as though for consolation over my apathy.

"What *are* you interested in?" he asked suddenly.

He'd shot the ball into the air. I waited till he caught it behind his back, and then said, "I've got my pet subject"—and I have!—"but at the moment I think I'm interested in this seamen's strike."

"Oh, is there one?" he asked.

"Just a small one!" I answered. "I hope it won't spread to the *Good Friday*." Evidently he didn't read the news, and imagined the world was just one big cricket field! I tried him on another item. "I see they haven't caught Cauldwell yet, the brickfield murderer," I said. "I don't suppose you got a copy of that latest edition the newsboy was rushing about with just as we left?"

"Ah, that's rather funny," he replied. "You see, I *did*. The only one, I think." He laughed. "Two people threw coins, but muffed the papers the boy threw back. They went in the water. Then I had a shot. I play cricket, you know. Biff, there goes the coin! Good catch. And here comes the paper!" He tossed his ball in the air and caught it. "Another good catch!" He patted his side pocket. "But I didn't know anybody had been murdered. In a cricket field, did you say?"

"No, a brickfield."

"Oh!" He wasn't interested. "I wanted to see what Port Elizabeth had made. 240 for six. Marks, 101 not out. You know, that chap's got a leg glide that I'll bet is as good as Ranji's. It's like—what?—a bird!"

Queer fellow. Rather pathetic. Then another queer fellow came along. At least, I thought it was a fellow, but it turned out to be a woman.

Well, now for my bunk.

*

Reason I haven't written lately is because one day is much like another at sea, I find. Same routine. Same food. Same people. Same games. Same view.

But to-day there's a change in the air—yes, in more senses than one.

First, the weather. It's been good, so far, but the glass is falling, and the Third Officer told me he didn't care for the look of it. Am not sure whether this was the sort of thing he should have said. To be truthful, I don't much care for the look of the Third Officer! I suppose he does some work, but he always seems to be poking around among the passengers, and with one of them in particular—Stedman, whose cabin's next to mine. Suppose he's all right, but don't care for him.

As a matter of fact, this morning I joined one of their conversations, which had to do with the second change in the air. That seamen's strike hasn't been left behind, after all. There's dissatisfaction down below, and trouble with the firemen. I was pitching into them, when Stedman rounded on me and told me they were underpaid, and were in the right. To my surprise, Brown—the Third Officer—seemed to agree. We might have had a row if Miles hadn't come along with his eternal cricket ball and scattered us by pretending to hurl it at us.

I shan't be sorry to get to England!

Yes, the more I think of that unknown spot I am going to, the more I like it. Haven House. A pleasant name. And this little niece of mine—whenever I take her photo out of my pocket, she gives me a friendly smile. Believe she's got a sense of humour. Hope so. Shall I walk in through the front door, or give her a surprise by creeping in through the wood at the back? Thoughtful of Henry to draw me that plan. "Essex isn't South Africa," he said, "but I'll be sorry to leave my little creek and wood and smooth lawns. You'll like it here, John." I think I shall, Henry. Poor old boy—I guess you've been better at home-making than I have. It will be pleasant to carry on for you. Silly of us to quarrel. I wonder what that little girl's voice is like?

⋆

Things are getting serious—including the captain's face. All sorts of rumours and counter-rumours going around. I even heard the word "Mutiny." Nonsense! Can't believe it! Anyhow, William Miles goes on playing with his ball!

Weather getting worse.

⋆

What is Brown doing in Stedman's cabin? Wish the walls were either thicker or thinner! If they were thinner, I might hear what they are saying, instead of this maddening, incoherent droning, and if they were thicker I couldn't hear anything at all!… Ha! That's stopped 'em! I knocked. Don't Third Officers ever go to bed?

It's been an uneasy day. I feel sure a lot's happening we're not being told about. Oh, well, go to sleep while the going's good!

⋆

Three men flogged this morning.

⋆

It's happened! But, even though my door is locked on me, I can't believe it! The thing's incredible!

Good Friday? I reckon this happens to be a bad one!

There was a *coup d'état* in the night. The whole thing must have been most devilishly well organised. There have been some casualties, I understand, and the ship is under the control of the mutineers. I got most of my information from a steward who is scared out of his life. The mutineers are armed. Brought the arms aboard. Brown and Stedman are in it, of course, and plenty of others.

The first thing they did, I'm told, was to smash up the wireless. Then they got out of hand and smashed everything else. The course is altered, and God knows where we are making for. South America, the steward thinks; but as he is in such a dither that he can hardly think at all, his opinion doesn't count for much! Most of the passengers are virtually prisoners—saving those, I take it, who have helped the Bad Cause. Why I didn't hear any of the fuss myself is due, probably, to my heavy sleeping, and the noise of the weather. The weather is getting worse and worse.

The steward says I was lucky to have slept through it. Some who didn't wish now that they had!

*

The best laid schemes of mice and men gang aft agley—or however the damn thing goes. The weather's winning, and the fools who thought they'd won are regretting some of their work! They did more damage than they realised, and we are now a crippled boat, with no means whatever of communicating our troubles to the outside world.

I ought to be scared out of my life. I can't make out why I am not. Maybe it's because the whole thing seems so grotesque and unreal—I'm still a prisoner, for the mutineers are afraid to let the passengers free—or maybe the condition of the steward makes me too contemptuous to risk dropping to his level. Nobody wants to die, and I'm sure I don't, but I have always felt that death is a vastly over-rated tragedy. Yes, I can think that even in the shadow of it. I said so to the steward.

"We're being driven south," he chattered.

"What's wrong with the direction?" I asked.

"It's out of every route," he answered.

"That'll save you a hanging," I said. "And here's a bit of advice from a prisoner to his jailer. Pull yourself together! We've all got to die once. And is the date so important? If we die now, it'll save us the inconvenience of dying another time."

The fellow seemed impressed with the idea. I had to feel a bit sorry for him.

"Yes—but what comes after?" he asked.

"I'm not a preacher, but I guess there's something," I said, "so put your house in order while there's time." Then I asked a question. Things were crashing above, and the ship seemed to be drunk. "What's the real position, steward? Are we in actual danger?"

He didn't answer. He just rolled his eyes.

"I see," I said. "And we're still to be locked in!"

He put his mouth close to my ear. "There's a man outside with a gun," he whispered. "If I don't lock you in, we'll *both* be shot!"

We heard a shot a moment later. He fled, locking the door violently. The boat is in the hands of madmen…

Whew! That was a lurch… Hallo—here's water coming in… My God!…

*

I did not think I should be writing again in this book. I don't know how many days have passed since I last wrote—we've all lost count of time—nor can I describe all that has happened. Sometimes events have been packed too closely to sort out any of them; at other times—just blanks. I don't even know who unlocked my cabin door when the ship became doomed. Brown says he did; but that may just be an attempt to whitewash himself. In the fantastic delirium that followed I found myself joining in the mad *suave-qui-peut* stampede, hugging a few possessions I never knew I had till afterwards, and somehow or other tumbling into a small boat with seven others. We got clear just before the *Good Friday* went down, and escaped the suction. Others weren't so fortunate.

The ship went down as the sun came up. The weather was so bad that we soon forgot everything but the job of keeping afloat. The fact that we did so goes to Brown's credit, anyway, and to the two sailors we had with us; but keeping afloat was all we could manage, and for an eternity the wind and the tide took us where they liked. Sometimes the eternity was black, sometimes grey. The sun that came out when the *Good Friday* sank soon went in again—it ought to have kept in for the sorry sight it shone on—and we haven't seen it since. But must we grumble? I suppose not. We've been sucked on to an island, and though our boat was smashed in the process, none of us were.

We've been here two days. The first day was spent mainly in panting and gasping. The second, more practically. We've collected most of the provisions which have been blessedly washed ashore, and we've reckoned up the food prospects on the island itself. We'll be testing some new diet before long—penguin pie, for one. Lawson swears he's seen a sea-elephant. That will be jolly—if we catch him! And there should be birds' eggs, fish, and something edible among the local vegetation. But, best of all, there's a stream. It tumbles down from the heights in the middle of the island and runs by the spot where we've pitched our camp.

So who's worrying?

*

Interruption. It's to-morrow. I had to turn out of my cave and do my bit—or several bits—wood collecting, food hunting, helping to get another barrel ashore, and tidying our three caves; also, organising a conference and trying to get tired minds interested. As matters are turning out, Brown and I are becoming the leaders of our party. I've an idea Brown is really ashamed of himself. Whether he is or not, it's a lucky thing we've got him with us. Incidentally, his watch is still going—he never forgot to wind it—he brought some useful things along with him, including an instrument or two, and the return of the sun has allowed him to get our bearings. Latitude 59.16 South and longitude 4.6 East.

And a lot of use *that's* going to be—as he remarked himself.

This is a small volcanic island, something of the type, I gather, of the Tristan da Cunha group. Precious little chance of being picked up—if any—but if we pull ourselves together and work out of our panic or lethargy, we ought to be able to live here till we can build a boat to get away in. That, of course, is our main task. It won't be easy, but it's got to be done.

The trouble is, we are not what you would call a picked lot! Though I am not as young as I was, I am one of the best. Brown is the most useful, and the two seamen, Bob and Jim, will be worth their salt—or penguin—when they've got over their demoralisation. I believe they're a bit ashamed of themselves, too!—as they damn' well ought to be.

The other four are pretty hopeless. One is the cricketer—who didn't leave his ball behind, and who is practising high catches at this moment. I am sitting in the entrance to my cave, and I'm not sure that I'm safe, for every now and then he hurls the ball at some imaginary wicket, and you never know where he's going to imagine it next! Another is Stedman, the man whose cabin was next to mine, and who was thick with Brown. He had a lot to do with that mutiny, I'll take my oath on that, and he's the one person who *doesn't* seem ashamed of himself. Unfortunately, he is sharing my cave. Brown and the seamen occupy one of the bigger ones, and Miles, Lawson and Jane are in the other. Lawson and Jane complete the eight of us. Lawson is a silly, weak-willed fellow, who keeps his mouth open and does what anybody tells him. He did what Brown and Stedman told him on the *Good Friday*. The throw-out of his family, I imagine. No brain at all. And Jane—odd, that our one woman should be Jane. She is the mannish-looking woman I mentioned in the first pages of this diary. She ought to be a beautiful girl, by the usual pattern of these things, whom the men fight for. Nothing of that sort. And yet—she has a curious attraction, and I've a feeling she will play her part—and that she's played it before. I'm sorry for you, Jane, but I don't much cotton to you... Still, we're not all made alike.

Whew! I just dodged it! *I* was the imaginary wicket that time, and the ball's gone in the cave! Here comes Miles, full of apologies.

Miles may be cracked, but he made a mad suggestion this morning that's going to prove useful. "I say, chaps," he said, over the meal we call breakfast, "what about a game of cricket to-day?"

At first he was laughed at. Then I realised the value of the idea. Keep us fit. Something to do. Change in our routine. Take our minds off ourselves.

"I'll play," I said.

"What with?" asked Stedman.

"I'll make a bat," said Miles.

We played in the evening. We all made ducks but Miles, who made 150 not out. The sea was six, but in future it is to count as caught, as penalty for the risk of losing the ball. Only four of us started playing, but the other four joined in before the end.

Sometimes, when I think of our ridiculous, hopeless position, I just don't believe it.

*

We've caught the sea-elephant!

*

I had a dream last night. Maybe it was the sea-elephant. If so, its dreams are sweeter than its taste. I dreamt I was arriving at Haven House. Dora was standing by a small white gate, with a basket of red roses. She was dressed in white. She threw her arms round me, and I carried her into the house, and then she sat on my knee… That's all. Sounds silly enough, but it was very nice.

Nicer than the reality I woke up to.

*

Made my first run. Then Jane caught me. Damn her!

*

This is the first time I've written for three weeks. I'm using up this book too fast. Odd, how values change. This book would be worth a penny in Cape Town, but here it's worth a thousand pounds. I've broken my pencil in two, so that if I lose one half I'll still have the other.

One reason I haven't written lately was to save space, another because nothing important has happened, saving the work on the boat and a century by Brown. Also, I've been too tired. To-day I feel a little fresher, however. That strange fish we had last night must agree with me. (It didn't agree with Arthur Lawson, who made terrible noises in the next cave all night.) And then it's my day off.

We've settled down by now into our routine, and accept it with few grumbles. We begin with a bathe, when the sea permits. Jane is responsible for breakfast and preparing all meals. After breakfast we work for four hours—the first shift. Brown supervises the boat-building, and allots the work according to the day's necessity and our particular skill, or lack of it. Any slacker goes without lunch. Afternoon, three hours. That's seven hours a day, and seven workers on the job. The eighth hunts for food—fish, penguin, eggs, a nameless plant we have found that doesn't kill us, and once a nameless berry that nearly did. We gave it several names after that. In the evening, cricket. Miles has carved some wickets on a slab of rock, and has made an excellent bat. He used valuable time doing it, but we let him. Atlantic Smiters *v.* Sea Dogs. I am a Sea Dog, with a top score of 7. Average 1.05. Miles inconsiderately keeps the averages. His is 82. He's the happiest of the bunch.

We work half-days on the days we think are Sundays, and once a fortnight each of us has a complete day to slack. This is mine.

Of course there has been no sign of a ship all this while. We are right round a corner of the world. We've managed to create some tools, and we salved all the nails off the original cases and barrels that came ashore with us. Brown has taught us a most ingenious riveting process, the nails, of course, not being enough. Smart chap, Brown. I've almost forgiven him. Wood's our difficulty. We go long expeditions for it. I spent one complete day getting a bit of wood equal to a small six-foot plank to the beach. Yes, this is work, and anxious work. But we're making progress, and this morning Brown told me cheerfully that we'll have the boat finished in another four months!

Socially we have merged better than, at first, I thought possible. Always with the exception of Stedman. Something very wrong about that fellow. He had to miss several lunches before he could be counted on to do his share, and even now he needs watching. Once he got ugly. The rest of us have fraternised, as fellow-sufferers should. We have forgotten a bad past in the very faint hope of a better future. One of our main jobs is to keep that hope from fading. Some of us seem to have lost a bit of heart lately. Lawson looks ill. I wonder what our condition will be like in another four months! Jane has kept up well. I am making no inquiries into Jane's private life. Miles lives for his evening cricket match. If ever I get back to civilisation, I never want to see a cricket ball again! Nevertheless, Miles's cricket ball, which has lost its original bloom, is proving a definite asset here.

Only why can't I make more than seven?

⋆

Another month gone by. I can only afford to write occasionally now. The blank pages are becoming scarce.

We are trying not to be too anxious, but we need more wood, and our health chart isn't good. Lawson seems to be giving out. One of the seamen was laid up for a week, and yesterday the other had a nasty tumble and hurt his leg.

Feeling a bit down to-day myself, but maybe that's just the result of three ducks running.

⋆

Nine!

*

I really don't know whether we're going to manage it, though we had a bit of luck a few days ago. Brown came across a tree we'd overlooked on the other side of the island. I thought he'd gone mad when he came bounding into our camp with the news. It's taken us most of the week to get the damn thing down and to cart it here in bits. We could have done it in half the time a month ago, when we had more strength. Diet's been a bit short lately. The penguins seem to have gone for a holiday. I think I'm getting a bit shaky myself, because last night, before going to sleep, I even forgot that I don't like Stedman, and talked to him as though he were a good companion.

"Going sick?" he asked.

That unusual solicitude began it.

"Can't afford to," I answered.

"Do you know you talked in your sleep last night?" he said.

I hadn't known, and I hoped I had not talked too much. I had not breathed a word to anybody about my secret. Still, in the circumstances, it was difficult to see how it was going to matter, either way.

"What did I talk about?" I asked.

"Gas," he said.

I think I was less disturbed at the fact that Stedman had heard about the gas than that I had talked about it. I usually have plenty of control, and this sleep-talking was not a good sign of my condition.

"I remember—I was dreaming," I lied.

Or maybe it wasn't a lie, only I did not recall the dream.

"In your dream," said Stedman, "you were pretty sick, because you'd only half-completed some formula or other."

I looked at him hard. He couldn't have invented that. And, as though to prove he wasn't inventing, he went on:

"And all at once you raised your voice and said, 'I must get there, I've got to get there—the money's just sitting there and waiting!'"

So I'd said that, too, had I?

"Well, it'll probably wait there till doomsday, as far as I'm concerned," I answered.

"Bad luck," he said. "I suppose you needed it to finish this formula?"

"Yes. I'm half-way to it, and the money would have allowed me to experiment till I'd gone the whole way."

"And then?"

"A fortune—for myself and my niece."

"Oh, you've got a niece?"

"She's the main reason for my going to England. Her father's dead, and I'm supposed to be looking after her."

"I envy you," he said. "I haven't any relatives, and can hardly remember those I had. Makes a man a bit lonely—and not too good company, eh? You get a bit hard, you know, when you've no one particular to care for—and no one to care for you. Lose interest in things. What's she like, this niece!"

I told him I'd never seen her. I showed him the photo. "I say, a stunner!" he exclaimed. "Yes, pretty bad luck to be on the edge of such good fortune, and then to have it snatched from you!" I answered. I began to develop self-pity. A thing I don't believe in. Another sign of the bad condition I'm in. I must watch myself. But Stedman was certainly showing a better side to himself, and I found it surprisingly pleasant to talk to him.

"Don't worry, it'll be all right," he said when I'd told him the whole position. "And if we *don't* finish the boat, then you can send your half-completed formula off in a bottle, so that some clever-shanks may pick it up and complete the other half!"

"He'd have to be a mighty clevershanks to complete it," I laughed. "Anyway, that formula doesn't leave the island unless I leave with it!"

"Oh, you've got it, then?" he said. "Well, hang on to it. You never know."

Then we said good-night and went to sleep.

I asked him this morning whether I'd talked any more.

"No, only snored," he replied. And then he added: "Look here, I'm odd man out here, I know that, but I'm not as bad as some of the folks think. If you can put in a word for me, I shouldn't mind."

"It's actions that speak, not words, Stedman," I told him. "If you want to get popular, you can do it."

Yes, but whoa! I must stop! I'm writing too much—this book's nearly finished. Only short entries in future, and only when I've anything special to say. Meanwhile, I must find some spot to hide this book, or Stedman will learn what I once thought of him!

*

Stedman improving. All agree. Jane made 13 to-day.

*

Ghastly thing happened this evening. We're still all nervy from it. We nearly lost our ball in the sea.

*

Brown says the work should be finished in a fortnight—if no one else goes sick. At one time we had Lawson, Bob, Miles and Jane all down together. I just hung out till Jane recovered, and then had a spell myself. Sort of fever gets hold of you. Weakens you.

But we'll do it.

*

Hit two boundaries running and then got a black eye.

*

The fortnight's up. About another week needed. Brown would have been right but for Jim's finger—the fool got a splinter in it, and it's gorn bad—and the time it took the others to recover. Lawson's still on his back, and, if you ask me, Brown himself ought to be. Stedman working like a horse. Jane doing pretty well, too. You can have as much private life as you like, Jane. I take off my hat to you! Funny, how your ideas of people change!

*

Penguins invaded us to-day. They wanted our camp; and, will you believe it, they nearly got it! We've the strength of a two-weeks' baby between the lot of us.

It was the cricket ball that gave us victory. Miles began throwing down penguins like wickets. The enemy retired with five casualties.

God, how I loathe penguin!

*

Finished! Finished! FINISHED! Now we've only got to find and get in the stores, wait for the right weather, and we're off! I think some of us imagine we'll meet a ship just beyond the horizon. Well, who knows?

*

Everything done! Just waiting for the tide. Brown gave out this morning. Suddenly collapsed, for the first time. He's the only one who never went sick. Expect it was reaction. He says he'll be all right, and will be able to crawl to the boat.

*

We leave in an hour. Stedman suggested a final game of cricket. We're so delirious that we all jumped at it. I think we're dotty. This little book has helped to keep me sane. If I *am* sane? We're going to play our last match of Atlantic Smiters *v.* Sea Dogs. The boat, all ready to start, will be just round Long Off Point. Miles swears he'll send a ball into it. It'll count 20. And afterwards, with the tide just right, we'll collect our final things, say good-bye to the camp, and... Ha! They're yelling for me!

*

Well—we played...

Miles hit his boundary into the boat. Stedman at long off, ran over the rocks to field the ball. He threw it back, but he didn't come back himself. He went off in the boat... And before he went—as I have just discovered—he rifled my pockets and stole my papers and my formula.

We shall never build another boat. There is no material left on the island. We are stunned.

Later. I have made another discovery—in a page of the newspaper that was tossed to Miles just as the *Good Friday* sailed, and that he has hogged in his pocket ever since so he could read the cricket news. He has read this news half a million times—never anything else. But the page that interested me contained a photograph of Stedman. Under it was: "George Cauldwell, wanted for the brickfield murder."

*

It is about two months since I last wrote. Yesterday we completed our monument, and to-day we all put our hands on it and took our oath. If ever we are rescued—in one year, two years, five years, ten years—we shall find you, Cauldwell, and save the hangman a job!...

Only one line left in book. Shall keep it, until...

*

At last! My God! My God! An empty boat...!!

CHAPTER XXVII

Conclusion

THEY FOUND A SHELTERED COVE ON THE SIDE OF THE ISLAND farthest from the camp, tucked *Spray II* in the least visible part of it, and waited.

They waited seven days. Then old Bob Blythe descended from the height on which he was taking his watch, tumbled into the *cayuca*, nearly upsetting it in his hurry, and rowed across the little strip of water from the shore to the yacht.

"She's comin'!" he announced hoarsely as he climbed on board. "I seen 'er!"

"Are you certain?" exclaimed Hazeldean.

"Certain? I'd 'ave know'd that boat without the telescope," replied Bob. "Didn't I ought?"

"And, besides, who else are we expecting?" added Kendall.

After that, no one spoke for several seconds. For a week they had been living with ghosts. Seven were ghosts indeed. But now the eighth had come alive, and was drawing nearer and nearer in solid, three-dimensional form. Even before his arrival, he projected an atmosphere which seemed as nauseating to Dora as that of the grave.

"Well, that's that," said Kendall suddenly. "Coming, Hazeldean?"

"Of course—if you're sure you've worked out the best plan," he answered.

"I'm quite sure of it. If it doesn't work, Bob knows what to do—only it's going to work. I always back my hunches. You're not forgetting, are you, that I am the only person here that our Mr. Stedman-Cauldwell hasn't seen? Don't worry, Miss Fenner. We'll be with you again shortly."

Then the *cayuca* returned to the shore once more, this time bearing Kendall and Hazeldean back to the island.

About two hours later, George Cauldwell, alias Stedman, alias Fenner, wanted in connection with the murder of ten people—one in South Africa, seven in England and two in France—stepped on to a shore of strange memories, and he stood quite still for awhile as the memories grew around him with painful vividness, seeming to bind his limbs with strands of the past. But though he was motionless, other figures flitted about. One was running towards a slab of rock, swinging an arm fantastically. Another, in front of the slab of rock, danced out and swept at space. Another came swooping towards the motionless spectator, who tried to move aside, but could not. The attempt was unnecessary. The swooping figure swooped right through him.

He tried again to move, and again failed. The spectral game continued, and held him. Once more a figure ran towards the slab of rock, stopping and whirling an arm twenty-two paces away; once more the figure at the slab danced out and slashed at the air; once more another figure came darting towards him, chasing something that moved faster... The thing that moved faster went plumb through Cauldwell's forehead.

Now he leapt in the air. The ghosts laughed, moaned, and vanished. He found himself in the midst of a terrible loneliness.

For years he had been lonely, since loneliness is the price of egotism and crime, the sour fruits of which provide no compensation. He had been lonely when he had fled from the police in Cape Town: one man against the world. He had been lonely on the *Good Friday*, while helping to deviate a course that would have led to the gallows. He had been lonely on the island, refusing at first to fraternise, and later fraternising with an evil purpose. He had been lonely after that purpose had been achieved. Dora Fenner had given him no love, for he had none to offer. His accomplices filled him with anxiety and suspicion, which accentuated his permanent background of fear; and when the nightmare of his fear actually came, he turned, as such men do, to the sole final refuge of physical comfort. This ephemeral refuge was supplied by Madame Paula. Now that was gone. The sea had even taken that in one of its own particular nightmares. It had nearly taken him, too; but not quite. His time was not yet. And here he was, through the doubtful grace of Brown's teaching—Brown—it was Brown who had been bowling last—yes, there he was again!—back at latitude 59·16S, longitude 4·6E—for what purpose?

"Yes—why am I here?" thought Cauldwell.

He tried to clear his mind, to remember. He had forgotten. He would have to wait till Miles hit the ball. No, it wasn't Miles this time, it was Jane. A queer person, Jane. But she had her uses. Not everybody had known Jane as Cauldwell had known her! And that young fool Lawson… Hey! She'd skied it! A catch!

He ran forward, his eyes towards the sky. The invisible ball descended into his cupped hands with a soft shuddering tickle. He stared at his empty hands. He took his handkerchief from his pocket and wiped his forehead.

"Why—am I—here?" he wondered.

He must know his reason! He'd had a reason! He would remember it in a moment. It was only that last storm that had disturbed his mind, making him forget things. That tumble down the hatchway, you know. Naturally, a bump like that…

"Ah! The diary!"

That was it! The diary! Of course. And when the complete world had turned against him, this island had also loomed as the only possible retreat. New memories might be created here, with Madame Paula by his side. He had painted the island to her in glowing colours as they had slipped away from the French coast. Glowing colours. Where were those glowing colours now? This grim, grey place… That he'd been trying to find again for weeks…

Come, come! Hurry!

Why hurry? What was there to hurry for? Where had he to get back to?

Weak in body through exposure and short rations, and weak in mind through lack of any mental nourishment, he moved across the haunted beach mechanically. He received a strange sensation as he did so. The ghosts had stopped playing, and were watching him, and as he crossed the pitch they turned in his direction and moved along with him.

"This is just imagination," he said aloud.

His voice was hoarse and unconvincing. He hardly recognised it. He wished he had not spoken.

Surrounded by the ghosts of those who had long waited for him, and with whose live bodies he had many times made this journey, he continued his mechanical progress across the beach. The ghosts became more and more insistent as he encountered evidences of their past existence. A broken wooden hoop, a bit of a barrel, a bit of split planking… rusty tins… a home-made hammer. He stooped over the home-made hammer, but did not pick it up. Soon, as he stumbled up the loose track, he stooped again. Footprints! He had not noticed these before. He turned and saw others, joining his own along the path he had come. The footprints of his invisible companions? He shuddered violently.

He came upon something else. His teeth began to chatter. It was the cricket bat.

How did the bat come to be here? Wasn't it down on the beach? He shook his head, to clear it. Things were growing more and more muddled in his mind. Of course, the bat on the beach was the ghosts' bat. He'd blow that away the moment he was himself again! Ghosts? Hell, everybody knew there weren't such things! But this bat here was real. This was the bat they had played with...

Yes, but how had it remained here? You'd have thought that fool Miles would have stuck to it as a memento!

Then another strange vision swept through the muddled mind of George Cauldwell, like a streak of revealing lightning in a chaotic sky. Beyond the rocky jut he was approaching were, he knew, three caves. Ghosts poured out of them, and came leaping towards him in violent spectral frenzy. Whish! They were gone! He even turned, to watch them vanish down the track to the beach, towards which was drifting the miracle of an empty but provisioned boat.

In that mad rush, much might be forgotten. A souvenir cricket bat, as well as a diary. In Cauldwell's own last moments on the island he had forgotten to search for the little note-book in which he had seen his fellow cave-mate writing, never thinking of it again until its existence had been indicated by the writer's final, uncompleted message in that gas-choked, shuttered drawing-room...

"Visions! Visions!" shouted Cauldwell. "Visions!"

They were trying to down him, but they wouldn't. He swept his arm round fiercely, to fight them off. The ghosts withdrew. He laughed derisively. They crept forward again. Again he lunged at them.

"Ha, ha!" he laughed. "Ha, ha! Ghosts and such hell bosh? I'll show you! Ha, ha, ha, ha, ha, ha!"

Violent with laughter, he went forward again. Once he nearly fell. Recovering his balance, he found himself standing before something he had never seen before. Here was no memory. Here was something completely new! His laughter increased in volume, to blot it out. The hysterical sounds ceased suddenly, as he read the words on the little rough monument that pointed skywards like an accusing finger:

FIAT JUSTICIA RUAT CÆLUM

It was a full minute before George Cauldwell's eyes became unglued from the inscription, and slid down to identify an object lying at the monument's base.

The object was a revolver. Whether he knew it was the revolver John Fenner had fired at him from the doomed drawing-room, missing him by an inch and hitting a picture instead—whether he even knew that his hand shot out, seized the revolver and pressed the trigger—will never be told, for now Cauldwell's brain snapped completely. And when Kendall and Hazeldean descended from their observation point, Cauldwell's earthly troubles were over.

"Well?" asked Kendall as he picked up the revolver and replaced it in his pocket. "Was I right?"

"I expect so," answered Hazeldean, hesitating. Then repeated: "Yes, I expect so."

They buried him underneath the monument.

That evening, in the midst of preparations for departure, Kendall suddenly asked:

"When are you two going to announce your engagement?"

Hazeldean glanced at Dora and laughed.

"I'm afraid it's too late," he answered. "We're married."

Kendall raised his eyebrows.

"Really? Why wasn't I told?"

"We didn't want you to feel *de trop*," responded Dora, "and—it was such fun cheating a detective!"

Then Kendall laughed.

"September 17th," he said, "at Freetown, Sierra Leone."